GHOST RIDER™

GHOST RIDER™

A NOVELIZATION BY GREG COX

BASED ON THE SCREEN STORY AND SCREENPLAY BY MARK STEVEN JOHNSON

POCKET STAR BOOKS
New York   London   Toronto   Sydney

An *Original* Publication of POCKET BOOKS

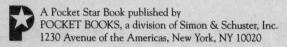

A Pocket Star Book published by
POCKET BOOKS, a division of Simon & Schuster, Inc.
1230 Avenue of the Americas, New York, NY 10020

This book is a work of fiction. Names, characters, places and incidents
are products of the author's imagination or are used fictitiously. Any
resemblance to actual events or locales or persons living or dead is entirely
coincidental.

ISBN-13: 978-1-4165-3818-9
ISBN-10:   1-4165-3818-6

This Pocket Star Books paperback edition February 2007

10 9 8 7 6 5 4 3 2 1

POCKET STAR BOOKS and colophon are registered
trademarks of Simon & Schuster, Inc.

Manufactured in the United States of America

For information regarding special discounts for bulk purchases,
please contact Simon & Schuster Special Sales at
1-800-456-6798 or business@simonandschuster.com.

It is said that the West was built on legends.
And that legends are a way of understanding
things greater than ourselves. Forces that shape
our lives. Events that defy explanation.
Individuals whose lives soar to the
heavens, or fall to earth.
These are how legends are born. . . .
—Roxanne Simpson, Southwest Cable News

GHOST RIDER™

Prologue

San Venganza, Mexico
1866

A FULL MOON SHONE DOWN ON THE RIDER AS HE GAL-
loped across the barren Mexican desert, astride a magnificent black stallion.

Coyotes, rattlesnakes, and other nocturnal predators
fled the sound of the pounding hoofbeats. A leather
duster and battered cowboy hat shielded him from the
chill of night.

Painful memories pursued the Rider, but he could
not outrun his destiny.

There must always be a Rider, Carter Slade knew. He
was only the latest mortal doomed to bear that curse.
Like all the Riders before him, he had made a deal, the
kind of deal you can't break. A deal with . . .

Mephistopheles.

In his mind's eye, Slade relived that fateful moment
when, in a burst of thunder and lightning, the Devil
had appeared before him in a desert much like this one.
A lean, shadowy figure, clad entirely in black, he had
leaned upon a cane as he'd arrived to claim Slade as his

own. A crystal skull had glittered upon the head on the cane, its skeletal grin mocking the doomed cowboy.

A second flare of lightning briefly exposed the demon's inhuman features: black eyes gleaming like polished obsidian from a cadaverous blue countenance.

Slade had known then that his mortal life was over.

To Mephistopheles, human souls were merely fuel for the hellish fires below. But the soul of the Rider was not like the others.

That night Carter Slade had become the Devil's bounty hunter, condemned to hunt down those who escaped from Hell. And to collect on the contracts signed over to his satanic master.

By contrast, Hell itself would have been a welcome relief.

The murky outline of ramshackle buildings appeared before him. Shaking off the tormenting memories, Slade forced himself to concentrate on the task at hand. He rode out of the desert into the town. Tonight his endless ride had brought him here, to the remote Mexican hamlet of San Venganza.

Tumbleweeds blew down the deserted streets of the village. Thick black smoke rose from the smoldering embers of burned-out buildings. More smoke billowed from the husk of the old Spanish mission at the end of main street. Soot stained the mission's whitewashed adobe walls. A bell pealed from atop the steeple. Acrid fumes escaped from narrow fissures in the dusty earth, as though there was an inferno burning just beneath the surface. The night wind carried the reek of brimstone.

The Rider trotted on horseback down the main street. Somber eyes surveyed the desolation, searching the doors and windows of the few surviving buildings for any signs of life. Wooden shutters swung open and shut in the wind, the mindless percussion matching the steady *clop-clop* of the horse's hooves. He passed the charred ruins of the general store, saloon, barber shop, hotel, assay office, and various mercantile emporia. False fronts, originally intended to make the rustic buildings look larger and more impressive than they actually were, now helped to conceal the full extent of the damage wreaked by fire. Iron bars in a window marked what was left of the town jail. An empty noose hung from the town's hanging tree. Spooked by the eerie scene, the midnight-black stallion trembled beneath the Rider. Its dark eyes were wide with fright.

"Easy, Banshee," the Rider said.

A singed piece of brown parchment was nailed to the door of the chapel at the mission. Slade nodded grimly at the sight.

Of all the deals ever made, no covenant was more powerful than the contract of San Venganza. Here an entire village had turned its back on God and signed over their immortal souls to Mephistopheles in exchange for worldly wealth and power.

But their newfound riches had not been enough for the corrupt villagers.

Consumed by greed and lust, they had turned on each other—until San Venganza drowned in its blood, leaving only these smoldering ruins behind. Overnight, the village had become a ghost town.

Now the souls of damned villagers were trapped here, waiting for the Rider to come and collect the deed.

Let's get this over with, Slade thought. Gripping the reins tightly with one hand, he rode the skittish horse up the steps of the ruined chapel and snatched the scrap of parchment from the door.

The scorching wind blew against his face, offering no relief from the stifling heat of the night, as it whistled through the empty street. The whistling grew louder as the wind picked up, taking on a moaning quality that sounded disturbingly human. He could practically hear the bloody chaos of the village's final days: men shouting, women screaming, gunshots blaring. The bodiless tumult filled the Rider's ears.

The horse whinnied in fear, almost bolting out from beneath the Rider. He pulled back on the reins, halting the horse so that he could listen more closely to the keening wind and the ominous sounds of the village. A door squeaked loudly as the wind tugged it to and fro on its one remaining hinge. A weather vane spun wildly atop the burned-out husk of the town hall. A clanging sound attracted his attention, and he peered at the dried-up well in the village square. A tarnished tin bucket hung on a rope over the well, banging against the stone housing as it swung back and forth, faster and faster as the wind wailed like a veritable army of lost souls.

The hellish cacophony was too much for the Rider's steed. Snorting and shaking its head violently, the terrified horse reared up on its hind legs. Its front hooves pawed wildly at the empty air. Frantic eyes rolled in their sockets. Steam jetted from its flaring nostrils. Froth flecked its lips. Banshee's agitated state said plenty about the evil that had overtaken San Venganza; this particular horse was no stranger to death and decay. It took a lot to frighten him.

The Rider tightened his grip upon the reins, fighting to bring the panicked horse under control. His other hand squeezed the rolled-up parchment—and a single drop of blood fell from the scroll onto the dusty ground.

"Steady, boy," he urged his steed, but the night continued its conspiracy to drive the horse nearly out of its mind. A swinging door squeaked, a shrill sound cutting through the darkness. Shutters clattered against their frames over and over. The church bell rang out hollowly. The metal bucket battered itself against the brick sides of the well, while, above everything else, the sulfurous wind shrieked like the damned. Noisome black fumes erupted from the cracked and barren earth. Fresh blood dripped from the dry brown scroll in the Rider's fist.

The tangy smell of the blood, on top of the noxious smoke and brimstone, only added to the stallion's alarm. Banshee worked himself into a lather. Striking hooves carved out deep divots in the packed ground as the horse reared up repeatedly, all but unseating the Rider. He grabbed onto the pommel of his saddle.

I've seen enough, the Rider decided. Tucking the bleeding scroll into his boot, he snatched a rawhide bullwhip from his saddlebag and cracked it loudly above his head. Silver spurs dug into the horse's sweaty flanks. *Time to get the hell out of here.*

Banshee hardly needed any encouragement. At a thunderous gallop, it raced out of San Venganza, leaving the accursed village behind. Dust clouds rose in the horse's wake. The echoes of the speeding hoofbeats soon died away.

Behind them, the smoking ruins of the dead village smoldered in the moonlight. The eventual crash of collapsing timbers went unheard. Nothing remained to watch the fiery ashes grow cold and still.

Nothing except for the moaning wind.

He found Mephistopheles waiting for him in the desert just outside the village. The Devil held out his hand, hungry for the thousand souls. His dark eyes gleamed in anticipation, as thunder crashed overhead and lightning flashed on the horizon.

No.

The power of the contract was so great that Mephistopheles must never get his hands on it, and damn the consequences. Carter Slade's own hand erupted into flame, instantly burning away his calloused mortal flesh. Bony fingers hung onto the contract, yanking it back from the Devil's fingers.

More flames spread over rider and steed alike, turning them into burning skeletons, aglow with hellfire. Cracking his whip once more, the Ghost Rider galloped away into the darkness, determined to do what only *he* could do: outride the Devil himself.

"*No!*" Mephistopheles raged. He limped forward on his cane, but the Rider was already beyond his grasp.

Slade heard the Devil's anger echo behind him as he rode like a phantom across the desolate moonlit wasteland. The tail of his long coat flapped behind him like a cape. He resolved to hide the dreadful contract somewhere far away, where Mephistopheles would never find it.

Carter Slade could never imagine that, many years hence, someone even worse than the Devil himself might come to collect.

1

THE TRAVELING CARNIVAL HAD TAKEN OVER AN ENTIRE vacant field outside Sweetwater, Texas. Calliope music competed with the excited squeals and laughter of the crowd thronging the midway. Sunlight poured down on garishly painted game booths and sideshow attractions. Popcorn and cotton candy scented the warm spring afternoon, tantalizing the taste buds of kids and adults alike. Brightly colored flags and banners streamed in the wind. Dating couples strolled hand in hand, while wide-eyed toddlers rode piggyback atop their parents' shoulders. Food stands hawked corn dogs, caramel apples, and funnel cakes. Carved horses pranced atop a spinning merry-go-round. A Ferris wheel offered a bird's-eye view of the entire county. Shooting galleries, balloon dart tosses, high strikers, and other (slightly rigged) tests of strength and skill offered teenage boys an opportunity to win various chintzy prizes for their dates. Lucky girls struggled beneath the weight of oversized stuffed animals. Unlucky boys blew more of their cash trying to win big. Canny game operators egged them on.

At the end of the midway, the big top lured hordes of fairgoers eager to see the carnival's star performers. Old Glory and the Texas state flag waved atop the voluminous orange canvas tent. A large plywood display, painted red and yellow to resemble a raging fire, framed the tent's entrance. Dozens of incandescent white lights formed block letters spelling out LEAP OF DEATH above the open threshold. THE AMAZING BLAZING STUNT CYCLE SPECTACULAR read the words alongside the entrance, accompanying painted portraits of two daring motorcyclists popping wheelies on opposite sides of the doorway.

"Step right up, ladies and gentlemen, boys and girls!" a carnival barker exhorted the crowd. "Don't miss your chance to witness the most death-defying motorcycle exhibition in the entire Lone Star State! Incredible thrills and a breath-taking display of cycling artistry, all for the price of admission. Get your tickets now!"

Dozens of small-town men, women, and children poured into the tent, filling the packed bleachers beneath the big top. The roar of a powerful motorcycle engine drew the spectators' gaze to a handsome teenage boy straddling a gleaming 750-XR Harley-Davidson at the top of a steep incline, which led down to the elaborate racetrack that had been set up in the center of the tent. The crisscrossing track doubled back on itself in an overlapping sequence of loops and curves, like a child's Hot Wheels set brought to life.

Pretty good turnout, Johnny Blaze thought as he appraised the crowd. A spotless white riding suit with bright red trim was fitted tightly around the seventeen-year-old's wiry body. A glossy white crash helmet shined beneath the spotlights. His sparkling hazel eyes searched the bleachers, looking for one very special face.

Johnny's spirit soared as he spotted her in the front row, smiling up at him from right behind the wooden railing. *There she is*, he thought excitedly. *That's my girl!*

As far as Johnny was concerned, Roxanne Simpson was the most beautiful girl in the world, or at least Nolan County. Long auburn hair framed her striking Hispanic features. Chestnut eyes threatened to swallow him up forever. A orange cotton tank top and tight denim jeans showed off her smooth, bronze skin and captivating figure. Lush pink lips cried out to be kissed. She was the single best thing that had ever happened to Johnny Blaze, and he knew it.

He winked at her before slapping down his face shield. Leaning forward on his bike, he gripped the handles and spun the rear tire just to warm up the rubber. *This one's for you, babe*, he thought as he kick-started the throbbing sport bike and took off down the ramp. The audience roared in approval, and Johnny imagined that he could pick out Roxanne's sultry voice from the general din. The 750's powerful V-Twin engine thrummed beneath him, sending him

11

from zero to sixty in a heartbeat. The furious growl of the "crotch rocket" drowned out the wind rushing past his helmet.

A second motorcyclist entered his peripheral vision, zooming up at him from the right as the two bikes sped towards the same intersection. Johnny didn't hit the brakes, slow down, or even flinch as the second bike whipped past him, almost (but not quite) cutting him off. Johnny barreled through the intersection without hesitation. He knew what he was doing—and so did his dad.

Barton Blaze's name was adorned on the back of his Kevlar-reinforced textile riding suit. His customized helmet and bike matched Johnny's own. Father and son chased each other around the circuitous track, missing each other by *inches* with every pass. The audience gasped at each near-collision, but Johnny figured he could do this routine with his eyes shut if he had to. After countless practice sessions, he and his dad had the split-second timing down to an art. Taking his eyes off the track, he snuck a peek at Roxanne as he zoomed past the lefthand bleachers. Her beautiful face, flushed with enthusiasm, thrilled him more than any death-defying stunt.

Keep watching, babe! I'm just getting warmed up. . . .

He slammed on the brakes, skidding to a halt at one end of the track. At the opposite end, twenty yards away, his father did the same. They faced each other across the length of the big top, gunning their engines in synch. Jump back in time several hundred years and they might have been dueling knights, preparing to joust.

Time for the big finale, Johnny thought. He glanced to his side, where a sealed propane tank was hooked up to the track. DANGER: FLAMMABLE read a warning printed on the side of the tank. He kicked a switch and watched as the fuel began to flow through a stretch of clear plastic tubing. He automatically checked out both the source and return lines, just like his dad had trained him to do. *Looks good to me. . . .*

A drum roll started up in the background, causing the crowd to hush in anticipation. A moment later, startled gasps broke the silence as the entire track suddenly burst into flame. Parallel streams of bright red fire traced the course of the motorcycle track, which suddenly resembled a speedway through hell. Johnny felt the heat of the flames through his insulated suit. The air above the track rippled like a desert mirage.

Johnny opened up the throttle and put the hammer down. Before the audience was done exclaiming over the flames, he charged the Harley right down the middle of the blazing course. Across from him, his father did the same, speeding straight toward Johnny. Heedless of the flames all around them, the two riders raced towards an explosive head-on collision. To the breathless audience, it looked like they were playing a deadly game of high-speed chicken.

Three . . . two . . . one . . . Johnny waited until the very last minute before climbing a built-in ramp and launching the Harley into air, at the exact same moment that his dad's bike took flight as well. Veering ever so slightly to the right, his bike flew past the oncoming motorcycle, the two choppers missing each other so closely that Johnny could feel the wind from his father's passage.

The crowd went wild.

The Harley's shocks absorbed the impact as he touched down back on the track. Johnny pumped his fist—the raucous cheers were like music to his ears as he pulled a wheelie, slipping the clutch to lift the front of his bike high into the air. Spotting Roxanne out of the corner of his eye, he took one hand away from the handlebars so he could wave at her. *Look, Roxanne! One hand!*

He was still riding one-handed when his rear wheel hit a patch of loose dirt. The bike started to slide out of control, right into the licking red flames, but Johnny threw his weight forward, dropping his front wheel back onto the track, only a second before he wiped out. The bike wobbled, but stayed upright.

That was a close one.

The audience hollered some more, perhaps thinking the near-accident was part of the act, but Johnny couldn't help feeling somewhat sheepish as he cruised out of the big top. He wanted to hope that maybe, just maybe, his dad hadn't seen the slip-up, but, deep down inside, Johnny knew better. He winced in anticipation of his father's response.

Man, am I going to hear about this one!

"You're a hotshot, aren't ya', boy?"

Barton Blaze wiped down a greasy connecting rod before placing it back on the work stand in front of him. No matter what else might be on his mind, he never cut corners when it came to inspecting and cleaning their equipment after every show. Pliers, wrenches, and other tools lay atop portable shelves and counters, alongside boxes of spare parts. A heavy-duty motorcycle lift suspended his own XR-750 above the ground. Wheel chocks waited to hold another bike in place. The cluttered interior of the maintenance tent smelled of grease, sweat, and motor oil. An air compressor hummed in the background.

"You're seventeen, you know everything there is to know, and you're going to live forever." The older man didn't look up from his work. His wind-burned features attested to years spent the riding the open road. Old scars hinted at the occasional spill. His wavy brown hair and rugged good looks still charmed the older women in their audience. "That about right?"

Johnny braced himself for the inevitable lecture. "Dad, it was just a patch of dirt—"

"That's not the point," his father began, only to be halted by a fit of deep hacking coughs. Placing his fist before his mouth, he struggled to catch his breath as he dropped down onto a stool in front of the bench. Barton's face turned beet-red. The convulsive coughs shook his wiry frame.

Alarmed, Johnny hurried forward from the crate he had been sitting on. *This doesn't sound good,* he thought. He reached out to assist his father, but Barton waved him away. Grimacing, the older man stubbornly got back on his feet all on his own. He immediately snatched a pack of cigarettes from the work stand and lit one up. He took a long drag from the cigarette as the coughing fit gradually subsided.

Slapping the crumpled pack back down onto the stand, Barton Blaze picked up right where he'd left off.

"The point is we've doing this act less than a week," he said, reaching around for a spanner wrench. Johnny grabbed the cigarette pack while his dad's back was turned, then furtively lobbed it into a nearby waste bin. "And *already* you're screwing around."

Johnny tried to appeal to his dad's showbiz instincts. "I was doing it for the crowd."

"We both know why you were doin' it." Lifting his gaze from his work, he saw right through Johnny. "She gonna stick by you when you're in a wheelchair? Huh?" His harsh tone rankled Johnny. "Huh, hot shot?!"

Johnny flashed his father a dirty look. How dare he suggest that Roxanne might desert him?! *We love each other . . . for real.*

"Everything you do in life, every choice, has a *consequence,*" Barton insisted. "When you do things without

16

thinking, then you ain't making the choice. The choice is making you." He shook his finger at Johnny. "Understand that?"

"Yeah, sure," Johnny mumbled. He just wanted to get this conversation over with. Roxanne was waiting for him.

"What?" his dad demanded.

Johnny stared at the floor. "I said, 'yes, sir.' "

His father nodded, apparently satisfied for the moment. Still puffing on his cigarette, he walked across the tented garage in search of a fresh rag. Johnny sullenly watched him while he waited to see if the dressing-down was well and truly over.

His restless gaze was drawn magnetically to the magnificent bike parked at the rear of the tent. *Ah, Grace.* An authentic 70s-era Harley-Davidson chopper, it had a classic yellow flame paint job over the midnight blue tank, a panhead Big Twin engine, a hard tail, and fishtail exhaust pipes. Chromed metal gleamed like silver. The front end of the bike was raked and stretched, seriously raising its coolness quotient. The elevated handlebars were almost, but not quite, ape hangers.

For maybe the millionth time, Johnny wondered what it would be like to cruise down the highway on the badass old-school chopper. "Dad?" he said hopefully. "I was gonna go for a ride." His eyes devoured the Harley's gleaming contours. He ached to climb into the blue leather saddle. "You think maybe I could take Grace?"

Barton shook his head, same as he always did. "Grace is a man's ride. Not a boy's."

Johnny bristled at his father's curt response. *I'm not a kid anymore,* he thought indignantly. *I'm almost eighteen!* Frustration churned inside him. *What's his problem anyway? I'm good enough to ride in the act, but not enough to trust with his favorite bike?* He opened his mouth to protest the sheer injustice of it all, but another voice spoke up first.

"Hey, Johnny."

He and his dad both turned their heads towards the open flap. Johnny's bad mood lifted instantly as he saw Roxanne standing in the doorway. Golden sunlight made her glow like an angel. Her sexy radiance took his breath away.

"Hi, Mr. Blaze," she said respectfully.

He nodded back at her. "Roxanne."

Johnny looked pleadingly at his dad, hoping to heaven that he wasn't grounded. As far as he knew, his father didn't have any problem with Roxanne herself, just the effect she had on his concentration. *Please, Dad. Let us have this time together.*

"Go on," his dad said gruffly.

Yes! Johnny thought, resisting an urge to pump his fist. He hopped onto his stunt bike and beckoned to Roxanne, who ran forward and mounted the cycle behind him. A smile broke out across his face as her arms wrapped around his waist. She pressed her warm softness against his back and he inhaled her perfume. He fired up the engine and the bike surged forward. They rolled out of the murky tent into the sunlight, leaving Johnny's worried father behind.

Roxanne's boisterous laugh rang out as they sped through the carnival outside. Strolling fairgoers hurried out of the way as the bike wove effortlessly through the crowd, easily dodging carnies and townies alike. Roxanne's long brown hair trailed in the wind. Johnny could practically feel her heart beating against his. Giggling in his ear, she playfully clapped first one hand, then the other, over his eyes.

"Hey, I can't see!" he objected, grinning the whole time. He pretended to snap at her fingers with his teeth.

"You're not missing any—" she began, then abruptly fell silent. Her fingers came away from his face and he felt her entire body tense up.

Oh crap.

A stout, middle-aged man stepped out into their path. An expensive suit and flashy jewelry betrayed both deep pockets and bad taste. A fuming cigar was clamped between his teeth. Apparently unconcerned by the oncoming motorcycle, he crossed his arms atop his chest and glowered at Johnny, daring the younger man to run him down. Johnny had no choice but to hit the brakes and slow to a stop. He threw the bike into neutral.

"Roxanne," Quentin Simpson said, no nonsense. A handlebar mustache and sideburns compensated for his receding hairline. His bulbous nose and sagging jowls made it clear that Roxanne had inherited her exotic good looks from her mother instead. Quentin's ruddy face bore a sour expression, and his tone equally brooked no disagreement. "You get off that bike right now, young lady."

A stony expression on her face, Roxanne didn't budge. She held on tightly to Johnny, while the Harley idled beneath them.

"I'm not going to ask you again," her father stated. His buffed leather shoe tapped impatiently against the floor of the midway as he puffed away on his imported cigar.

"Go, Johnny," she said, defiance rising in her voice. She rested her chin possessively upon his shoulder, like she wasn't going anywhere.

Johnny didn't know *what* to do. Part of him was proud that she was willing to stand up to her father for him. On the other hand, he didn't like coming between Roxanne and her family. Johnny already knew that he wanted her to be part of his life forever, so it seemed important that he treat her father with respect. After all, if Johnny's dreams came true, he was going to have to deal with Quentin Simpson for years to come. He looked squarely into his prospective father-in-law's eyes, man to man.

We can work this out. I know we can.

Mr. Simpson sneered at the teenager behind the handlebars. "Everyone has a station in life, son. You and your old man work for a carnival. I happen to *own* the carnival." He dismissively looked Johnny over. "What do you have to offer my daughter but grease under your nails and life in a trailer park?"

"I love her," Johnny proclaimed. What else mattered?

The carnival owner snorted. "You're a *phase*, son. Just a phase."

The words stung Johnny more than he wanted to admit, even to himself.

Roxanne nudged him with her chin, urging him to take her away from here. Conceding defeat, at least where winning her father's respect was concerned, Johnny put the bike into gear and swerved around Simpson. Spinning tires churned up the sawdust beneath them as the bike tore out of the carnival and onto the open road. Roxanne choked back an angry sob and hung on to him with all of her strength, pressing herself so hard against his back that it was difficult to tell where she ended and he began.

Johnny silently cursed Roxanne's father for upsetting her like this. *Forget about me*, he angrily thought. *How can he treat his own daughter so harshly? Can't he see how happy we could be together?* It's not like Roxanne and her dad were particularly close; Quentin mostly ignored her when he wasn't cracking the whip. It was Johnny who had helped Roxanne get through her parents' messy divorce by being there when she needed someone to talk to. That was how their romance had begun. He had understood what she was going through. In a sense, they had both lost their mothers. Johnny wished he could do something to make Roxanne's problems go away, but all he could give her right now was a sympathetic shoulder to cry on and a temporary escape from her father's domineering ways.

That was going to have to be enough, at least for the moment.

Fortunately, he had the rest of his life to give her all the love he had.

Or so he hoped.

2

J & R Forever

Johnny carved the crude prophecy into the bark of a majestic oak tree. The oak crowned the top of Crowley Hill, a grassy mound overlooking fields of fragrant Texas bluebonnets. Rolling prairies stretched out for miles around. Fluffy white clouds drifted through a peaceful blue sky. The raucous clamor of the carnival, and Quentin Simpson's scornful voice, seemed very far away.

The teenage boy put the final touches to the inscription, then stepped back to inspect his work. *Looks good to me.* He smiled at the thought of he and Roxanne returning to this spot, many decades from now, to find their initials still linked together on the old oak's trunk. *How cool will that be?*

He closed his jackknife and tucked it back into his rear pocket. Turning away from the tree, he found Roxanne standing a few feet away, staring out over the fields of flowers with a sad, distant look on her face. He came up behind her and gently wrapped his arms around her waist. Sighing, she rested her weight against him.

"What's wrong?" he asked.

Roxanne shook her head, not wanting to talk about it. Her pensive gaze drifted out to the endless blue sky. Several moments passed before she finally said what was on her mind.

"I'm leaving."

Johnny blinked in surprise. "What?"

"My dad's sending me to live with my mom."

His heart sank. "When?"

"Soon," she said glumly. Johnny could tell she was just as dismayed at the prospect as he was. Maybe even more so.

Anger flared inside him. He knew exactly what Quentin Simpson was up to. "He's trying to keep us apart."

She turned to face him. Dark eyes glistened moistly and a teardrop traced it way down her cheek. Her mournful expression tugged at his heart. She reached up and clasped her hands behind his neck, holding him close. "So what do we do?"

"We'll leave," Johnny said defiantly. A sense of resolve came over him. There was no way he was going to let Roxanne's tyrannical father come between them. "We'll jump on the bike and we'll just keep going. . . ."

Hope flickered upon Roxanne's face, followed immediately by a worried look. She looked up at him with concern. "What about your father?"

"He doesn't need me," Johnny said, his mind made up. "He doesn't need anybody." Barton Blaze had been a carnival star for years, before Johnny joined the act; he could always perform solo again if he had to. Johnny remembered his father's stern words earlier this afternoon, and decided that he could live without the frequent nagging and lectures. *Maybe it's time to strike out on my own. Show him that I really am not a kid anymore.*

But when to make their escape? Johnny was tempted to take off with Roxanne right this second and never look back, but common sense dictated that they prepare first. He needed to go back to the fair to pack some clothes, cash, and personal belongings, and Roxanne doubtless needed to do the same. If they were really serious about leaving the carnival behind forever, they had to do this right.

"Tomorrow," he decided. "Noon. We'll meet here."

Roxanne nodded and rested her head against his chest. They held onto each passionately, not ready to leave this place, until a sudden wind whipped across the hilltop, shaking the branches of the sturdy oak and rustling the grass around their ankles. Lifting his eyes to the horizon, Johnny was surprised to see dark clouds racing towards them. Lighting flashed in the distance, followed by the rumble of far-off thunder.

Roxanne shivered in his arms as the cold breeze chilled her tender flesh. The baleful black clouds obscured the sun. Goosebumps broke out across Johnny's skin.

A storm was coming.

Racing trophies and old circus posters decorated the interior of the Blazes' trailer. One poster showed Barton jumping his cycle through a ring of fire. Another showed him flying the bike over a gaping canyon. Brightly colored type touted THE AMAZING BLAZE! ONE NIGHT ONLY! while an equally garish banner ballyhooed THE LEGENDARY LEAP OF DEATH! A map of the continental United States was mounted on one wall. Colored tacks indicated every small town and city the show had ever played in. After decades on the road, the faded map looked like a pincushion.

Walking on his tiptoes, Johnny quietly closed the door behind him as he entered the trailer. If he was lucky, he could pack up his things tonight without his dad catching wise. Storm or no storm, Johnny was determined to ride away with Roxanne tomorrow, right before the afternoon matinee. He wanted to be halfway to New Mexico before both their fathers even realized they were gone.

Loud snores came from the living room. Creeping toward his own bunk, Johnny saw that his father had fallen asleep in his overstuffed easy chair. Barton Blaze's chin drooped onto his chest as he slumped in the chair. A ratty blue bathrobe was draped over his slumbering body. For a moment, Johnny was surprised by just how frail and tired his father looked. Strands of gray had infiltrated his light brown hair. When did the Amazing Blaze get so old?

Looking more closely, he saw an open photo album resting upon his father's lap. A family photo, taken back when Johnny's mom was still alive, was neatly taped onto the exposed page. In the photo, a much younger Barton was proudly holding up his son, while his wife looked on with a gentle smile on her face. Circus pennants fluttered in the background. Grace, his dad's beloved chopper, looked brand new.

Johnny's throat tightened. His mother had died when he was very young; he couldn't even remember when that photo was taken. For a moment, he felt guilty for planning to run out on his dad. It had always been just the two of them, for pretty much his entire life. His resolution faltered . . . until he remembered Roxanne's tearful face looking up at him beneath the sheltering oak. *It has to be tomorrow*, he reminded himself, *before Roxanne's dad can send her away.* He felt bad about leaving his dad alone like this, but what other choice did he have? Besides, it wasn't like this wasn't going to happen someday anyway; he had to set off on his own some time. *This is my chance. Maybe my only chance to be with Roxanne forever. I have to go for it. It has to be now.*

Or risk ending up old and alone like his father.

A glint of crinkly aluminum foil caught Johnny's eyes. Looking down, he spotted that same open pack of cigarettes resting in his father's grasp. *Guess I didn't get rid of those after all.* Clearly, he had underestimated his dad's need for a nicotine fix. Johnny smiled ruefully as he gingerly extracted the pack from Barton's fingers and looked around for the wastebasket. *If at first you don't succeed . . .*

The overflowing wire basket sat on the other side of the easy chair. Johnny walked around to once more dispose of the cigarette pack. A crumpled letter lay atop the trash. Johnny stopped in his tracks as he glimpsed the word "hospital" in a fragment of the note's letterhead. He quietly lifted the letter from the garbage and smoothed it out so that he could read it. The full letterhead read *St. Michael's Mercy Hospital. Abilene, Texas.*

What the . . . ? Abilene was only an hour away from here; the carnival had played there last weekend. He hastily skimmed the note, his heart plunging as the pitiless phrases leaped out at him:

. . . chest x-ray indicates several large masses . . . cancer has spread . . . have left you several messages but have not heard back . . .

Johnny felt like he'd been run over by a truck. Tossing the letter back into the trash, he dropped limply onto the vinyl couch across from his sleeping father. He stared numbly at his dad, trying to make sense of what he had just learned. *Cancer?* He winced at the memory of his father's ugly coughing jag earlier that day. *I should have realized that something was wrong with him! How could I have been so blind?*

The sight of the half-empty cigarette pack resting atop the wastebasket enraged him—if looks could kill, Johnny's furious glare would have set the murderous "coffin nails" afire. He cursed himself for not trying harder to get his dad to kick the habit. Why hadn't he forced his dad to quit?

Despair crashed down on him as he realized that there was no way he could run off with Roxanne. He couldn't leave his father now, no matter how much it cost him personally. As much as he loved Roxanne, his dad needed him more.

Johnny leaned forward, resting his head upon his hands. In an instant, his dreams of happiness with Roxanne had gone up in flames. He groaned out loud, accidentally waking his father. Barton stirred within chair. His bleary, bloodshot eyes found his son.

"What time is it?" he asked.

"It's late," Johnny said, unsure of what else to say. Should he let on that he knew about the cancer? He wondered when his dad was planning to tell him about his illness. A selfish part of him wished that he had never seen that goddamn note, that he and Roxanne had made a break for it while they'd still had the chance. Now it was too late for both of them.

"Where ya' goin'?" Barton called after him. Another coughing fit struck without warning, causing Johnny's dad to double over in his chair. He pressed a soiled rag to his lips while he hacked up a load of bloody phlegm. Crimson spots showed through the fabric.

"Nowhere, Dad," Johnny murmured, more to himself than his father. The aluminum walls of the trailer closed in on him like a prison. "I'm going nowhere."

A thunderbolt split apart the night sky as carny roustabouts scurried to strike the tents before the storm hit. Tarps went up over the carousel and other rides. Food stands and game booths were battened up. Hanging strings of twinkle lights added a deceptively festive flavor to the scene.

Amidst the bustling activity, no one noticed a solitary stranger strolling down the deserted midway.

Mephistopheles took his time, unconcerned by the approaching tempest. Tall and deathly pale, he calmly took in the sights and sounds of the unraveling carnival. His long black coat flapped behind him like a magician's cape. Yellow hair, the color of fool's gold, was slicked back away from his high forehead. He walked with a slight limp, the legacy of a bad fall a long time ago, and he swung a polished silver walking stick before him. A crystal skull, its vacant sockets gaping above a skeletal grin, adorned its top. The macabre ornament reflected the twinkling lights strung along the midway.

Walking past the various rides and sideshow booths, he paused in front of the carnival funhouse. A cartoon devil, complete with horns and pitchfork, was painted above the funhouse entrance. A forked tail and hooves completed the portrait.

Amused, Mephistopheles chuckled quietly to himself before continuing on his way. The lights on the midway blinked out, one by one, as he passed beneath them, creating a path of pitch-black darkness in his wake.

Johnny puttered inside the maintenance tent, doing nothing in particular. Unable to sleep, he had also been unable to bear the claustrophobic atmosphere of the trailer a minute longer. Looking over the stunt bikes, just to make sure they were ready for tomorrow's performances, gave him an excuse to get out and be alone with his thoughts, if only for an hour or so. *How can I explain to Roxanne that our plans are off?* he fretted. For all he knew, she was furtively packing her things at this very moment. *Could she ever understand why I can't leave with her now?*

A sudden chill descended over the garage. His goose bumps returned as the temperature inside the tent seemed to drop fifty degrees in a matter of seconds. Johnny's breath frosted before his lips and he stared dumbfounded at the icy puffs. *What the hell?* he thought in confusion. Storm or no storm, this didn't make sense. *It's August in Texas, for God's sake.*

"Johnny Blaze."

Still puzzled by the inexplicable cold snap, he turned to see a stranger standing in the doorway, exactly where Roxanne had been several hours ago. A long black coat cloaked the mysterious figure's bony frame. Dark blue eyes seemed to shimmer in the darkness, like a cat's.

Jeweled rings glittered upon his fingers. More gems studded his shirt and sleeves. Although he looked to be in his sixties, the man had a full head of bright blond hair.

Johnny was pretty sure he had never seen this guy before.

"Yeah?"

"I caught your show today," the stranger said. His mild voice had a cultured air. "I wanted to tell you how much I enjoyed watching you ride."

"Oh," Johnny replied uneasily. Maybe he was just another autograph seeker, but he was getting kind of a creepy vibe from the guy. "Thanks."

He turned back toward the bikes, hoping that was all the stranger wanted.

"Perhaps you'll ride for me someday," came the reply.

A job prospect? This piqued Johnny's interest. No matter what happened with his dad, he certainly wouldn't mind getting out from beneath Quentin Simpson's thumb, and the sooner the better. "You run a show?"

"The greatest show on earth." The stranger gave a sly, cryptic smile, as though indulging in a private joke. The chill permeating the air suddenly ran through Johnny's blood. Even though he didn't know this guy from Adam, the brief idea of possibly working for this spooky dude made his skin crawl. His foggy breaths hung between them, and it occurred to Johnny that the freaky cold snap had arrived at the same time as the stranger. Maybe Quentin Simpson wasn't really so bad. . . .

"What's wrong, Johnny? Worried about your father?"

Johnny's jaw dropped. "What do you know about that?"

"Like I said, I was at the show," the stranger replied with a shrug. "A blind man could see he's sick." Johnny relaxed a little. The man's explanation sounded plausible enough. "What is it? His heart?"

"Cancer," Johnny whispered, speaking the dreaded word aloud for the first time.

"I'm sorry," the stranger said with genuine concern. "Of course, the worst part with cancer is the time it takes. The toll on the loved ones." My God, it was almost like he could read Johnny's mind. "Lives are altered. Plans are thrown off course. . . ."

Johnny grimaced as the mystery man's words hit home. *Roxanne,* he lamented, feeling his heart crack in two. *We came so close.* Once her father sent her away, he might never see her again. What if she met someone else while she was living with her mom?

The stranger studied Johnny's expression. His feline eyes seemed to peer into the teenager's anguished soul. "I'm moved by your devotion, Johnny." He twirled his cane before him. "What if I could help your father?"

"Yeah?" Johnny blurted, praying that the stranger wasn't just messing with his head. Was he a doctor or something? Maybe a specialist with some experimental new treatment. "How?"

"How's not important. If I could make him better, just like this."

He snapped his fingers.

"Give him back his health."

Snap.

"Give you your freedom."

Snap.

"Would you be willing to make a deal?"

Lightning flashed outside. In the sudden glare, the crystal skull seemed to have changed subtly. Its death's-head's grin looked wider and more malevolent. The gleaming teeth seemed longer, almost like fangs. Thunder rumbled nearby.

Johnny swallowed hard. This whole thing was like some corny old horror movie, but he didn't feel like laughing. *Is this is for real?* Part of him wanted nothing to with the mysterious stranger—but if there was even a chance that the man could do what he said . . .

The words came out before Johnny even realized he had spoken.

"Name your price."

The stranger smirked, obviously pleased by the young man's answer. Raising his left hand, he swept his finger along the line of motorcycles parked against the tarpaulin. He dragged out his words as he did so.

"I'll take . . ." His pointing finger lingered on Grace. ". . . your soul."

Johnny laughed out loud, suddenly struck by the sheer ridiculousness of the situation. *What was I thinking?* he asked himself, embarrassed by his own momentary gullibility. Doctor Strange here was obviously some kind of a nutjob.

The stranger didn't seem to mind being laughed at. Maybe he got that reaction all the time. "By sunrise to-morrow, your dad will be as healthy as a horse . . . and you will have your whole life ahead of you." He reached into his coat and extracted a rolled-up paper scroll, which he held out to Johnny. Heavy brown parchment crinkled as the stranger unrolled it for Johnny's inspection. "It's your choice."

Johnny's laughter died upon his lips. He warily eyed the expensive-looking sheet of parchment. Paragraphs of handwritten text were inscribed upon the document, but Johnny couldn't make out what they said. *Is that Latin?* Try as he might, it was hard not to take this peculiar business seriously. *What if this guy isn't crazy?*

Slowly, he reached out for the paper. His fingertips grazed the edge of the document, which seemed to twist beneath his touch, giving him a nasty paper cut. He hissed in pain and a single drop of blood leaked onto the parchment before he jerked his hand back. He looked down at his wounded finger. A thin scarlet line sliced across his stinging flesh.

"That'll do just fine," the stranger said. He took back the blood-speckled paper. The thunder boomed overhead as the storm finally struck with full force. The deafening blast jolted Johnny—

—who sat up abruptly in bed.

Whoa! He looked around in confusion. The shadowy maintenance tent was gone, replaced by the familiar sights of his own room aboard the trailer. Sunlight filtered in through the window curtains. Blinking to clear his eyes, Johnny glanced at his alarm clock. It was almost ten AM, and the stranger was nowhere to be seen.

"Damn," he murmured. *That was one hell of a dream.*

Throwing on some clothes, he staggered from his room and headed for the door. He looked around for his dad, but Barton Blaze was nowhere to be seen. Reality loaded down Johnny's shoulders as he recalled everything he had to deal with today. He wanted to think that his dad's cancer was the stuff of nightmares, too, just like that creepy stranger, but he knew better than that. It was time to face the inevitable—his father was dying, and so were Johnny's dreams about Roxanne. *I need to find her. Tell her that our plans are off.*

He wasn't looking forward to the conversation.

As he emerged into the bright Texas sunlight, however, he was surprised to find his father energetically washing the outside of the trailer. A bucket of soapy water rested on the ground by his dad's feet, while the senior Blaze sprayed the trailer's corrugated aluminum wall with a hose, rinsing off a thick layer of suds. He whistled a cheery tune as he worked, looking more hale and hearty than he had in months. Seeing his father like this made Johnny realize just how depleted his dad had been lately.

Until now.

Barton spotted Johnny. "Well, if it isn't Sleeping Beauty," he said with a grin. His blue eyes twinkled. His face had a rosy glow. Despite his strenuous exertions, he wasn't even breathing hard. He lowered the hose to avoid soaking his son.

"Dad . . ." Johnny didn't know what to make of his father's seeming recovery. "You look . . ."

"Great, right?" He chuckled at Johnny's bewildered expression. "Least that's what the doc said this morning when he looked at my X-ray."

Johnny struggled to keep up. "You went to the doctor?"

"I've been sick, son." His voice took on a more serious tone. "And now that I finally got the nerve to tell you . . ." Unable to contain his joy, he shook his head in disbelief. A broad smile broke out across his face. "Well, I'm not anymore."

Dazed, Johnny stared speechlessly at his father.

An overwhelming sense of relief warred with a creeping sense of dread. The stranger's words whispered at the back of his brain.

By sunrise tomorrow, your dad will be as healthy as a horse. . . .

But that was just a dream.

Wasn't it?

3

JOHNNY HURRIEDLY STUFFED SOME SPARE TOOLS INTO A bulging duffel bag. He had already packed his clothes and worldly possessions. Now he just needed to borrow a few bike parts from the maintenance tent, in case he and Roxanne broke down somewhere on the road. He promised himself that he would pay his dad back as soon as he found a paying job outside the carnival.

A glance at his wristwatch revealed that it was almost noon. He mentally kicked himself for sleeping the whole morning away. *Roxanne's waiting for me. We should have been on the road by now.*

After all the unexplainable weirdnesses of the last several hours, there was only one thing he knew for certain: he and Roxanne were in love. Now that his father wasn't sick anymore (God only knew why), their plan to run away together was back on. Johnny wanted to escape the fairgrounds before his dad found out what was up. He hastily zipped up the duffel bag and strapped it onto the back of his Harley.

Too late. Just as he was starting to climb onto the

bike, the canvas door flapped open and Barton Blaze stepped into the tent, all suited up for this afternoon's death-defying performance. "Biggest crowd of the week!" he said exuberantly.

Caught up in his own high spirits, he didn't pay close attention to Johnny at first. He searched a cluttered shelf for his black leather riding gloves. "You know what I was thinking about? A new stunt. One that will put us over the top." Finding his gloves tucked in between a toolbox and can of WD-40, he started to put them on. "A jump, me from one side, you from the other. Only instead of cars, a helicopter, its blades spinning." He stretched his fingers to make sure the gloves were in place securely. He turned toward Johnny. "Whattaya' think?"

He blinked in surprise as he noted that Johnny wasn't suited up for the show. "Boy, you got about two minutes to get into your suit or . . ." His voice trailed off as he spotted the packed duffel bag strapped to rear of the bike. His jaw fell open as comprehension dawned in his eyes. In one of the few times that Johnny had ever known, Barton Blaze was absolutely speechless.

Johnny tried to explain, fumbling for the words that refused to come. "Roxanne . . . her dad is sending her away." He prayed that he could make his father understand. "If we don't leave now, it will be too late." Barton stared numbly at his son, his weathered face unreadable. "It's like you said. Make my own choices . . ."

"You do this," his father rumbled, finally finding his

voice, "it'll have consequences that last the rest of your life. It only takes a moment to turn, but a lifetime to turn back."

"I wouldn't go," Johnny insisted, "if I wasn't sure you were going to be fine."

His father shook his head. He wasn't having any of this. "Two kids on the run with nothing . . . if your goal is to end up together, that's a great way to make sure as hell it *doesn't* happen!"

What was his dad implying? That their romance wasn't strong enough to survive a few bumps in the road? A surge of resentment stirred inside him; he couldn't believe that his dad had so little faith in his and Roxanne's feelings. This was no silly high school crush. It was the real thing! Why the hell couldn't he see this?

"I'd rather take my chances with her than spend my whole life jumping bikes at some stupid carnival!" he barked. "I want something better than that!"

Johnny regretted the words the moment they burst from his lips, but there was no taking them back. Not now, not ever. He could only stare at his father's crushed expression and feel like the lowest of the low. He looked away from his dad, unable to meet his eyes.

"Her old man will have the cops on you before you reach the county line," his dad murmured in a defeated tone. All the forcefulness had been leeched from his voice, replaced by a mournful resignation. He dropped down onto a stool.

Johnny guiltily turned back toward his bike. There seemed nothing more to say. He glanced around the maintenance tent, making sure he hadn't forgotten something. *At least Dad's not sick anymore.* There was still time to make it up to him sometime in the future. Right now, though, he had to focus on Roxanne and getting the hell out of here.

"Hey, hot shot." Johnny was surprised to hear his dad call out to him. He looked over at Barton, who lobbed a set of keys at him. Johnny snatched them out of the air, then peered down at the keys in his palm. He instantly recognized the keys to Grace. Johnny looked up at his dad and smiled. He realized that this was the closest thing to a blessing he was ever likely to get. "Take Grace. At least you'll have a decent head start."

Johnny gave his dad a grateful look. Despite everything, he knew his father loved him.

I won't forget this.

"Ladies and gentlemen, the Amazing Blaze Stunt Cycle Spectacular!"

The barker's amplified voice rang out over the fairgrounds as Johnny prepared to make his departure. He glanced back over his shoulder at the big top, then revved Grace's engines. Twelve hundred cc's of raw power sprang to life beneath him, eager to hit the open road. Grace had a full tank of gas, which would be more than enough to carry Johnny and Roxanne beyond her father's suffocating grip . . . forever?

Maybe . . . maybe not.

He took one last look around the carnival, feeling a sudden pang of nostalgia for the life he was about to leave behind. Most kids dream of running away to the circus, he reflected; how ironic was it that he and Roxanne were doing exactly the opposite? Smiling sadly, he listened to the excited cheers coming from inside the main tent. The audience's collective oohs and aahs were as familiar to him to as a childhood lullaby. *Sounds like Dad's blowing their socks off,* he thought with pride. He kicked the bike into gear and started away from the tent.

Without warning, a tremendous crash came from behind him. From the big top. Johnny froze at the unmistakable crunch of mangled metal. The crowd's enthusiastic cheers and gasps gave way to horrified screams.

Dad!

Johnny wheeled Grace around, skidding to a stop. He leapt from his seat, letting the precious Harley topple over onto the sawdust. A mass of confused townies blocked the entrance to the big tent. Johnny shoved his way through the milling rubes, not letting anything get between him and his father. He rushed into the tent, where his anxious eyes confirmed the awful truth.

Barton Blaze lay amidst the flaming tracks. His wrecked motorcycle rested on its side several yards away, its wheels still spinning. Shaken men and women fled the bleachers, holding their hands over their chil-

dren's eyes, while others in the audience stood transfixed by the shocking tableau before them. Barton's fel-
low performers looked on in dismay. A pale-faced
trapeze artist called frantically for a doctor.

"*Dad?!*"

Ignoring the helpless spectators, as well as the flames
running along the length of the track, Johnny raced to
his father's side. He jumped over the fiery display,
barely feeling the heat. Dropping to his knees, he cradled his dad's head upon his lap. Cracks and skid marks
scarred Barton's crash helmet.

"*Somebody call an ambulance!*" Johnny hollered at the
top of his lungs. He searched his father's face, looking
for some sign that his dad wasn't hurt as badly as it
looked. Barton had survived some nasty tumbles before—that was just part of the biz. Yet this crash looked
worse than any he could remember.

"Johnny . . . ?" Barton said weakly. His blue eyes
struggled to focus on his son. He lifted a trembling arm,
trying to reach out to Johnny, but his strength was fading fast. The arm dropped limply onto the track. Blood
trickled from the corner of his mouth.

Barton Blaze was dying . . . again.

"Dad!" Johnny blurted hoarsely. Hot tears streaked
his cheeks. "It's going to be okay. I'm here." The memory of their last painful encounter tore at his heart. "I'm
not going to leave, I promise." He grabbed onto his father's hand and squeezed it. Gloved fingers were too
weak to squeeze back. His dad's eyes lost their focus.

44

His breathing grew shallow as his throat rattled. "Dad? . . . Dad!"

A final shudder passed through Barton Blaze's body before he fell forever still. Glassy eyes stared blankly into eternity.

No! This can't be happening. Sobbing, Johnny clutched his father's lifeless body to his chest. He pleaded silently for God to restore his father to life, but heaven's mercy seemed very far away. Unable to accept that his father was beyond help, he looked desperately at the entrance to the big top. *Where the hell is that ambulance? Why won't somebody help me?*

His frantic gaze locked on a solitary figure limping calmly toward the exit. A long black coat and silver cane identified him as the mysterious stranger from the night before. Unlike the other aghast audience members, he looked not at all alarmed by what had just transpired. As Johnny stared in shock, he strolled casually out of the tent—the stranger might have been leaving a chamber music recital, not a horrible human tragedy.

Johnny couldn't believe his eyes. What was the hell was *he* doing here? Johnny had half-convinced himself that last night's unsettling visitor had been nothing more than a figment of his nocturnal imagination. But that was no dream that had just slipped out from beneath the big top. The stranger was real—and so too perhaps was the unholy bargain they had struck in the murky confines of the maintenance tent?

I don't understand. He said Dad would be okay. He promised!

He gently lowered his father's head down onto the floor of the track. The flames surrounding them sputtered and died away as someone finally thought to shut off the gas. Not quite knowing why, Johnny jumped to his feet and took off after the enigmatic stranger. Well-meaning carnies tried to offer their condolences, but he didn't have time for that right now. Brushing their kind words and offers of help aside, he tore out of the tent onto the midway.

Outside the big top, a funereal pall was already falling over the hectic fairgrounds as news of the fatal accident spread through the crowd. The amusement rides slowed to a stop. Twinkling lights switched off. The sideshow barkers halted their spiels. Numerous hushed conversations supplanted the screams of laughter. Sympathetic eyes turned toward Johnny, but he wasn't even aware of the pitying gazes coming at him from all directions.

Instead, he desperately scanned the midway for the elusive stranger. Wiping the tears from his eyes, he looked all around, but the mystery man was nowhere to be seen. *He couldn't have gone far, not with that bad leg of his!* His eyes peered through the packed bodies crowding the fairgrounds, looking in vain for any trace of a long black coat or swept-back blond hair. But he might as well have stayed beside his father's body.

It was as if the stranger had vanished into thin air.

• • •

Less than an hour later, Johnny was tearing down a lonely country road outside of town. Grace rode like a dream, but that did nothing to dispel the boy's anguish.

Heavy black storm clouds blotted out the sun as he sped past empty plains guarded by miles of barbed wire fences. A longhorn steer skull, bleached white by the sun, hung upon a fencepost as Johnny zipped past the bovine death's-head at over one hundred miles per hour. A hot wind blew against his tear-stained face, ruffling his hair. His crash helmet was left behind, laying forgotten in a tent somewhere.

But as fast as he rode, he couldn't outrun the searing memory of his father's death—and the sheer injustice of it all. *He wasn't sick anymore*, Johnny thought furiously. *He was going to live!*

Fresh tears momentarily blurred his vision . . . until a white-hot lightning bolt struck the road directly in front of him. The report of thunder boomed overhead.

In the sudden glare, the stranger was now standing right in the middle of the road.

Oh hell.

There was no time to apply the brakes. Reacting quickly to avoid hitting the stranger, Johnny was forced to lay Grace down onto the pavement so that the Harley skidded across the asphalt on its side, sparks flying where the chrome and titanium met the road. As Grace came screeching to a halt, Johnny was thrown clear of the bike, hitting the blacktop hard enough to break every bone in his body.

Or so he thought.

Stumbling to his feet, Johnny was stunned to find himself more or less intact. He stared at his arms and legs in confusion, seeing only a few minor cuts and scrapes. *I don't get it.* If not killing him, that tumble should have at least put him in an ICU, especially with no helmet on. But all he seemed to need was a Band-Aid or two.

He looked about him, realizing for the first time that he had been about to zoom through a crossroads without even glancing for oncoming traffic. The stranger leaned on his cane at the center of the crossing, smirking at Johnny.

"You're no good to me dead."

The stranger's sardonic tone enraged Johnny. Forgetting all about his miraculous brush with death, he wheeled around to confront the older man. He threw out an accusing finger.

"You killed him!"

He didn't need to explain who he meant.

"I cured his *cancer*," the stranger said. "That's what I promised. That's what I did." He shrugged his shoulders. "The rest I left up to you."

What? Is it really my fault that Dad died? The horrible thought had been lurking at the back of his mind ever since the accident. Had their fight in the tent upset his father, enough to make him lose his concentration just when he needed it most?

And worse, was that what the smirking stranger had planned all along?

"You son of a bitch!"

Johnny charged. He grabbed for the other man, intending to tackle him to the pavement, but, all at once, the stranger wasn't there. Johnny's arms closed on empty air and he stumbled forward, almost falling onto his face. At the last second, he managed to hang onto his balance and he spun around to find that the stranger was now standing behind him. His startled eyes bulged from their sockets.

How . . . ?

"One day," the stranger said, "when I need you, I will come. Until then I will be watching." More thunder rumbled on the horizon. A solitary windmill spun its blades. Buzzards circled overhead.

"Forget about friends. Forget about family." He reached out and laid his hand upon Johnny's shoulder. An icy chill spread through the teenager's bones, freezing him in place. Johnny tried to pull away from the stranger's touch, but his body refused to cooperate. "Forget love."

Roxanne . . . ? What about her?

"You're mine, Johnny Blaze."

A torrid wind whipped up the dust at Johnny's feet. The whirling sand enveloped him, forcing him to close his eyes against the barrage of tiny particles. The stranger withdrew his hand.

The dust devil dispersed as quickly as it had appeared. Opening his eyes, Johnny found himself sprawled upon the pavement, right where he had crashed before. Grace lay on her side several feet away. Just like last night, it was as though this latest confrontation had never occurred.

Empty roads stretched out before him. Johnny was alone at the crossroads, with no one else in sight for miles around. Once again, the stranger was gone.

But his parting words reverberated in the young man's memory.

You're mine. . . .

Roxanne was waiting under the old oak tree, just like she promised. Johnny saw her standing atop Crowley Hill, looking as fantastic as usual. Her auburn hair and chestnut eyes filled him with a hopeless yearning. He longed to bury himself in her arms. With his father dead, she was all he had left.

And yet he had to let her go.

No love, the stranger had warned him. Did Johnny have any choice but to take that injunction seriously? His brief dealings with the sinister black-garbed man, whose true name and nature Johnny shrunk from thinking about, had already cost his father his life . . . and Johnny his future. For Roxanne's sake, he couldn't allow her to become trapped in the stranger's web of death and deception. Johnny knew he'd never forgive himself if something terrible happened to her as well.

She spotted him as he rounded the bend on Grace. She waved at him excitedly, practically jumping up and down in her eagerness to start their new life together. Her gorgeous smile broke his heart.

Just like he was about to break hers.

He slowed to a stop at the bottom of the hill, treating himself to one last look at the best thing that had ever happened to him. Somehow he knew that no matter what became of him now, no matter how many years and miles he put between them, he would never find another woman who would touch his soul the way Roxanne had. She was one of a kind.

She still beckoned to him from atop the hill, looking slightly puzzled as to what he was waiting for. Her light brown eyebrows arched quizzically and her incandescent smile went down a few watts. She started down toward him, unwilling to wait any longer.

Johnny knew he had to leave before she joined him. Once she was in his arms again, her shining eyes and lips only inches from his own, there was no way that he would ever be able to say good-bye to her for good. If he wanted to get away, spare her from the nightmarish purgatory his life had become, he had to go now, right this very minute.

He tore his gaze away from her breathtaking beauty and put Grace into gear. The Harley accelerated beneath him and he hammered down the road, leaving Crowley Hill behind. Sneaking a peek at his wing mirror, he saw Roxanne standing speechless upon the lonely mound. He caught only a glimpse of her stricken expression before her figure shrunk out of sight.

The woman he loved disappeared in a cloud of dust.

His heart ached, but he knew that he had made the right decision. Someday the stranger would return. When that happened, Johnny wanted Roxanne Simpson to have no part in whatever was in store for him.

It's better this way.

Light and hope faded from his eyes as Johnny stared grimly into the horizon.

An endless road stretched before him.

4

Present Day

HAUNTED EYES STARED THROUGH THE FACE SHIELD OF a sturdy crash helmet. The tinted plastic visor reflected a sea of spectators packed into the bleachers surrounding the El Paso motor speedway. Floodlights lit up the infield area in the middle of the oval racetrack. The bright lights overpowered the starry night sky overhead, not that anyone was looking up. Thousands of eager fans awaited the appearance of their idol. Concessions workers trotted up and down the steps of the bleachers, hawking cold drinks, Popsicles, and snacks. Fat cats and celebrities lounged in air-conditioned comfort in reserved luxury boxes, while regular folks and their kids crowded the cheap seats. Camera crews stood ready to record the event for the cable sports channels. Anticipation filled the air as the moment of truth drew near. Rising to their feet, the audience chanted in unison.

"BLAZE! BLAZE! BLAZE!"

For a moment, Johnny was transported back to his carefree days under the big top. Before the stranger . . .

and the Accident. Now in his thirties, Johnny performed in larger venues these days. A white synthetic riding suit fit snugly onto his lean, muscular physique. Crimson flames were emblazoned onto the suit and matching helmet. The Plexiglas visor hid the emptiness in his eyes.

He sat astride a throbbing XR-750. Painted flames embellished the sport bike's pristine white finish and shining chrome. His gloved hands gripped the handlebars as he contemplated the jump before him. Thirty-five hard-body trucks were lined up side-by-side between the take-off ramp in front of Johnny and the landing ramp on the opposite side of the track. All in all, he was looking at a jump of over fifty yards with nothing but several tons of heavy metal to cushion his fall if he came up short.

In other words, the usual.

Time to give the folks a show, he thought. He pumped his fist in a move that was now copied by hero-worshiping school kids all across the country. Right on cue, the row of trucks burst into flame. Fiery orange tendrils reached for the sky, throwing off so much heat that Johnny could feel the warmth all the way through his protective garments. High-decibel southern rock cranked from the speedway's blaring public address system. Over thirty thousand screaming spectators roared in approval. The warm summer night smelled of gasoline and adrenaline.

Johnny cracked the throttle and the 750 accelerated

up the ramp at breakneck speed. He waited until the very last second before tapping the nitrous oxide button to give the bike the extra boost it needed to take off into the air above the burning trucks. A battery of flashbulbs went off in the stands. The crowd was on its feet. . . .

High above the artificial inferno, time seemed to stand still for Johnny as he and the bike arced across the sky. His eyes closed and a rare look of serenity came over his face. Moments like this, when the line between life and death was as thin as a narrow strip of speeding rubber, were the only times he ever felt truly free.

Not even the stranger could touch him now.

Too soon, however, the soaring bike began its descent. Johnny opened his eyes and realized at once that he given the engine a little too much nitrous. The bike was flying too far, so that he was going to overshoot the landing ramp by several yards. A collective gasp came from the audience as they reached the same horrifying conclusion. Nothing but solid blacktop awaited the diving bike and its rider.

Looks like I'm in for a nasty spill, thought Johnny, oddly unafraid. Taking a deep breath, he braced himself for impact as he passed over the landing ramp, only seconds before the sport bike crashed nose-first into the asphalt. Fireworks, preset for the finale, ignited on both sides of the ramp, throwing geysers of white sparks into the air. The force of the landing threw him from the saddle. He tumbled across the speedway into the concrete retaining wall protecting the audience from the racetrack. His helmet's heavy-duty face shield shattered like glass. Johnny grunted in pain, his outburst drowned out by the terrified screams of the spectators. His entire body slammed against the concrete. He slid onto the ground, lying flat upon his back.

"Johnny!"

His chief mechanic was first on the scene. Randall "Mack" Mackenzie came running across the speedway, breathing heavily. A short, stocky man wearing an oil-stained T-shirt and jeans, he stared wide-eyed at Johnny's body. Beneath his brown beard, his face had gone white with fear. For all he knew, his best friend and employer wouldn't be getting up again.

Ever.

Mack dropped to knees in front of Johnny. Trembling fingers hurriedly pried Johnny's crash helmet away from his skull, exposing a mop of untidy black hair. If the injured rider was aware of his friend's presence, he gave no sign of it. Johnny's chin drooped onto his chest. Only the whites of his eyes were visible.

"C'mon, J.B.," Mack pleaded. He patted Johnny's cheeks, trying to get a response. "Talk to me . . ."

Johnny heard Mack's voice coming from what seemed as if very far away. The distraught gearhead sounded as if he was rapidly running out of hope. Floating in darkness, barely feeling his injuries, Johnny felt himself slipping away . . . until another voice surfaced from his memory.

You're no good to me dead.

The welcoming darkness receded as his aching flesh and bones called him back to the mortal world. Johnny's eyes rolled forward. He blinked and looked around.

"Is the bike okay?" he asked.

Mack let out an enormous sigh of relief. He wiped the cold sweat from his brow. "He's fine," he called out to the rest of Johnny's stunt team as the men caught up to them by the retaining wall. An ambulance raced toward them, its flashing lights and siren going full tilt. Mack grabbed a first-aid kit from one of the newcomers.

His buddy wanted to start patching him up right there, but Johnny figured he owed the crowd a better finale than that. "Give me a lift," he instructed his men, over Mack's useless protests. Johnny winced as the crew helped him to his feet; his ribs felt badly bruised. He waved at the audience, reassuring them that he was all right. A thunderous cheer erupted from the bleachers. Johnny briefly wondered how many of the spectators thought that the crash was all part of the act.

Applause followed him across the speedway as he made his way toward the Team Blaze tour bus parked right outside. Every step sent another jolt of agony through his aching ribs, but all his working parts still worked. Mack kept shaking his head, like he couldn't believe that Johnny was actually walking away from a fall like that. Johnny just hoped that someone was looking after his bike.

Looks like I live to jump another day. For whatever's that worth.

As they left the speedway, his men had to clear a path through a frenzied throng of fans, groupies, and autograph seekers. The excited horde crowded the stunt team on both sides, jostling each other in their eagerness to catch a glimpse of the world-famous Johnny Blaze. "Johnny! Over here, Johnny!" they shouted at him, trying to get his attention. "Remember me, Johnny?" Posters, magazine covers, and publicity photos were thrust at him, but Johnny hurt too much to sign anything right now. Brazen women called out their phone numbers, or tried to slip a note to his body-guards. A sultry young Latina bore a superficial resem-blance to Roxanne, as she'd looked so many years ago, and a familiar pang stabbed at his heart. He hadn't laid eyes on the real Roxanne since the day his father died. . . .

A TV news crew elbowed their way through the fans to meet Johnny right in front of the bus. A logo on the camera identified the crew as belonging to ESPN2. The reporter, whose name Johnny couldn't recall, stepped forward.

"Johnny, you gave us quite a scare." He shoved a

microphone in Johnny's face. "What happened out there tonight?"

Johnny walked past him without a word.

The tour bus rolled down the moonlit highway. A trademarked flaming banner adorned both sides of the deluxe land cruiser. Vanity plates read BLAZZZE-1. Mesquite and yucca sprouted alongside the road, which stretched across hundreds of miles of inhospitable desert. Sparse vegetation rarely grew higher than a man's waist around these parts. Prickly pear cacti and tumbleweeds dotted the barren wasteland. A Texas-shaped road sign was posted along the highway. DRIVE SAFELY, the sign exhorted. THE TEXAS WAY.

Inside the bus, the crew passed the time on the way to the Dallas-Fort Worth metroplex. Most of men played poker around a long table, laughing over cigarettes, nachos, and longneck beers. Playing cards were slapped onto the table, to be greeted by muttered curses and triumphant chuckles. Plastic chips clattered as they passed from one cardplayer to another. ZZ Top blared from the bus's sound system. Tobacco fumes and dirty jokes filled the air. A television set, the audio muted, was mounted above an open doorway. Coverage of this year's X-Games flickered upon the screen. Freestyle BMXers flipped their bicycles backwards and forwards in the air. Others performed outrageous stunts on ramps and trails.

The crew cheered the best cyclists on.

A few yards back from hilarity, Mack and Johnny shared a booth at the rear of the cabin. A martini glass full of jelly beans—Johnny's only vice—rested on the table between them. The mechanic's eyes were glued to the screen of his handheld PlayStation Portable, where a computer-generated facsimile of Johnny was attempting to recreate one of the real Johnny's most spectacular jumps: a double rollover launched from a curved fiberglass ramp. Mack's fingers and thumbs feverishly worked the console's controls, but not smoothly enough. The CG rider missed the landing ramp by a mile, crashing upside-down onto the pavement in an explosion of fiery red pixels. An unnervingly realistic-sounding crash came from the PSP's sound chip, followed by an urgent voice that Mack was rapidly coming to hate:

"And Blaze is down!"

So what else is new? Mack silently groused. The game, a complimentary copy of *Johnny Blaze—Airtime!* had been kicking his butt for the last one hundred miles or so. Despite his best efforts, he couldn't get past level one. *Who designed this stupid game? The Devil himself?*

He looked across the booth at the real Johnny Blaze, who was engrossed in a paperback copy of Zane Grey's *Riders of the Purple Sage*. On the cover of the book, a lone rider galloped a spotted Appaloosa across a windswept prairie. The dog-eared paperback showed signs of heavy wear; Johnny had always had a weakness for classic westerns.

"This game is impossible," Mack complained.

Johnny glanced up from his book. A narrow cowboy hat rested upon his head. He shrugged once, then turned another page. Apparently settlers and range riders in 1870s Utah were more compelling than his best friend's mortal combat with the fiendish computer game.

Mack hit replay. On the game screen, the CG Johnny gunned his engine and sped toward the take-off ramp. Mack stared at the screen intently, the glow from the console lighting up his face. He struggled with the virtual clutch and throttle, trying to keep the miniature cycle on track. This time he triggered the Launch command a few seconds later, only to find himself overshooting the landing ramp—just as Johnny had done for real. Another electronic crash sounded from the PSP. The CG Johnny tumbled headlong over the handlebars before smacking into the pavement.

"Oh!" the invisible narrator exclaimed. "That one's gotta hurt!"

The audio mayhem pulled Johnny out of his book. He arched an eyebrow. "Have you tried *not* crashing?" he asked wryly.

"Have *you*?" Mack shot back.

Before Johnny could return to his paperback, ZZ Top fell silent as somebody switched the TV off mute. Mack looked up to see a color photo of Johnny upon the screen. He nudged Johnny, who turned around in time to catch what appeared to be some kind of TV profile.

"Here at the X-Games," a sportscaster declared, "we've seen big air, big moves, and, of course, big crashes." A montage of gravity-defying bicycle stunts flashed across the screen. "But ask all these riders who it is they look up to, and the answer is a man who's not even competing here."

The film clips were replaced by a series of talking heads belonging to various young daredevils.

"Johnny Blaze," the first Extreme biker said. A caption identified him as *Travis Pastrana*.

"Johnny Blaze," one Mike Metzger stated without hesitation.

"Watching him is what got most of us hooked on bikes in the first place," Nate Adams insisted. "He's the best!"

Footage of some of Johnny's most famous stunts played upon the TV screen. A perilous leap over a pit filled with hissing rattlesnakes. A loop-the-loop executed at over a hundred miles an hour. Riding a tightrope over Niagara Falls. Zooming through over a dozen flaming hoops at Madison Square Garden. Jumping from the top of one skyscraper to another. Racing around the rim of the Seattle Space Needle. Climbing the elevated ladder of a fire truck into a burning building—and out the other side. The "Pit and the Pendulum" stunt, with Johnny narrowly missing a swinging blade while catching air over a bottomless chasm. Weaving through a staged stampede of longhorn cattle. The rocket-powered launch over Copperhead Canyon . . .

Each clip evoked a vivid memory for Mack. He remembered every heart-stopping moment. He figured he lost a year of his life, and a layer of stomach lining, every time Johnny had a close call. It was a miracle his hair hadn't turned completely white by now.

"He's been called the 'the Father of all Moto-X,'" the sportscaster continued. "He's revered by riders all around the world, despite the fact that he's always shunned the spotlight, refusing to do any interviews. His personal life is a mystery, the man himself an enigma even to his fans." The reporter pressed a microphone on the trio of extreme bikers from before. "Why is he the name on everyone's lips?"

"Skills. Creativity," Mike explained. He doffed his backwards baseball cap in respect. Johnny's face was tattooed on his arm. "But if I had to say what sets him apart from everyone else . . . *the guy has no fear.*"

Nate nodded in agreement. "No fear whatsoever."

"Even when a jump's getting away from him," Travis said admiringly, "he's got this look like . . . like he doesn't care what happens to him."

Tell me about it, Mack thought. Sometimes he wished Johnny had a healthy dose of fear in him, not to mention the slightest bit of interest in his own self-preservation. Most of the time, actually.

But then he wouldn't be Johnny Blaze. . . .

Fresh footage, of that crash landing earlier tonight, ran on the TV. Mack winced, and the guys around the poker table groaned in sympathy, as Johnny slammed into the retaining wall in front of thirty thousand horrified fans. The visor on his helmet exploded outward in slow motion. The shaky video clip, which looked like it had come from some spectator's camcorder, threw Mack back to those awful minutes immediately after the crash, when it had really looked like Johnny wasn't going to make it.

That was the worst crash yet, he thought, *and I've seen some beauts.*

Spotting the remote on nearby counter, he clicked off the TV. Nobody objected; Mack guessed that the rest of the crew had found the crash footage just as disturbing as he had. No one aboard the bus was in any hurry to relive that incident just yet. The guys gratefully returned to their game as the conversation turned back to booze, babes, and whose hand was it anyway? Cards were shuffled and cut.

Mack plopped himself back down in the booth. He looked across the table at Johnny. His face held a disapproving expression.

"What?" Johnny said finally, conscious of his friend's scrutiny.

Mack didn't mince words. "You should be takin' a dirt nap after that rag doll today."

"I got lucky," Johnny said.

Mack wasn't buying it. " 'Lucky'? My hunting dog's named Lucky and he's got one eye and no nuts." He didn't expect his words would have any effect on Johnny's reckless behavior, but he had to make the

64

effort, if only for his own piece of mind. "Lucky don't cover it, J.B. You got an *angel* watching over you."

"Yeah, maybe," Johnny murmured. A pensive look, that Mack knew too well, came over his friend's face. A melancholy tone entered his voice as Johnny turned his head to stare bleakly out the window at the forlorn desert outside. The tinted window reflected his brooding demeanor. "Or maybe it's something else."

Like what? Mack wondered, but he knew better than to press Johnny when he got into a mood like this. He had known Johnny Blaze for years now, and was the closest thing the celebrated rider had to a confidant, but there were times when Mack felt he didn't know Johnny at all. All he knew was that his friend carried some sort of terrible burden with him wherever they went. Mack had given up trying to figure it out. *He'll tell me about it when he's ready . . . if he lives that long.*

Outside in the darkness, the desert held its own secrets.

The bus rolled on down the highway, leaving an isolated stretch of badlands behind. Creosote and cacti cast their shadows onto the arid landscape. A coyote howled mournfully at the moon, while other nocturnal predators prowled the darkness. A murder of crows perched upon the gnarled branches of a mesquite tree.

A wind picked up from out of nowhere, stirring up the dust. The crows cawed in agitation, then took off into the sky, abandoning the desert wasteland as quickly as their wings would carry them. Skunks and lizards scurried for cover. Lightning lit up the sky and thunder rumbled.

Polished black boots stepped confidently onto the dry soil. They strode briskly across the desert, without a hint of a limp. A youthful hand reached down and scooped up a clot of dirt. A silent figure ran the loam through his fingers, sampling it the way a prospector would. The loose soil seemed to meet with his approval.

Cold black eyes—a hunter's eyes—surveyed the desolate landscape. His gaze darted from right to left, scrutinizing his surroundings as though witnessing them for the first time—which indeed he was.

So this is the world, he thought. A night-flying owl swept down from the sky and carried off an unwary jackrabbit. The youth savored the small mammal's terrified squeals. *It shows promise*.

He watched the raptor and its prey disappear into sky. Icy stars glittered overhead. The vast immensity of the heavens, so very different from his native realm, filled him with a sense of keen anticipation. He was eager to set his plans into motion. He had lofty ambitions where this benighted plane was concerned, and much to accomplish before he fulfilled his unholy destiny. His father would not be pleased, but what did that matter? His reign would soon be over. A new era was nigh.

Let it begin, he resolved, *so that my hour might come round at last*.

A jagged thunderbolt split the night. The sudden glare cast the figure's lean shadow across the barren wasteland.

A heartbeat later, the shadow was gone.

And so was the figure.

5

It was well past midnight by the time the bus dropped Johnny and Mack at a nondescript corner of downtown Forth Worth, across the street from a run-down Texaco service station. Towering glass monoliths loomed over several blocks of sweatshops, stockyards, and warehouses. This time of night, there was nobody around to see the two men push the mangled remains of the stunt bike up an alley running past a two-story brick warehouse. Mack wasn't sure he could salvage the wrecked motorcycle, but he wanted to give it a try. If nothing else, he might be able to cannibalize the bike for spare parts.

Waste not, want not, he thought. One never knew when a spare valve or crankshaft might be needed. *Especially at the rate Johnny chews up motorcycles.*

A service elevator carried them up to the loft that served as Johnny's home—when he wasn't touring, that is. As usual, Mack was struck by the way the line between garage and apartment had been completely erased here. Over a dozen motorcycles, along with assorted tools and spare parts, were scattered throughout the loft, amidst the couch, bar, pool table, and other furnishings. Harleys, Hondas, Triumphs, Yamahas, Vulcans, and Suzukis were all represented in Johnny's collection. Red brick walls surrounded a gray cement floor. Painted black columns held up the ceiling. Carnival posters hung upon the walls. Rubber tires were piled up in one corner. A box of pistons waited to be unpacked. Greasy rags were draped over doorknobs.

Stepping out of the elevator, Johnny dropped his duffel bags onto the cluttered area of hardwood floor. Mack wheeled the trashed bike into the living room, parking it next to the entertainment center. The bike's kickstand had snapped off in the crash, so he had to lean it up against an empty stretch of wall. He shoved a couple of heavy cinder blocks against the wheels to hold it in place until he had chance to take a closer look at the damage. Not tonight, though. He was too pooped.

Mack glanced around at the garagelike ambiance. The distinct odor of motor oil hung in the air. "Said it before, I'll say it again. This place could use a woman's touch."

"So could you," Johnny teased his friend. He strolled into the kitchen, which was located on a low mezzanine overlooking the main floor, and poured himself a fresh martini glass of jelly beans from a plastic canister. Clearly, Johnny's sweet tooth had come through the accident intact.

I do all right, Mack thought indignantly. *Sometimes*.

Glancing around the loft, the mechanic's gaze settled on Grace, occupying a position of honor in one corner of the living room. The venerable Harley, which hadn't been ridden in years, had definitely seen better days. A thick layer of dust dulled the chopper's blue-and-yellow paint job. The chrome was nicked and scratched in a dozen places. Rust ate away at its chassis. Both tires were flat. The corroded chain looked dry as a bone. Duct tape patched up tears in the leather saddle.

As a motorcycle lover, Mack was always pained by Grace's sorry state. It was a crying shame that such a fine machine should be neglected like this. Still, he knew that Johnny had his own reasons for wanting to leave Grace alone, even if he also couldn't bring himself to get rid of his father's bike. A framed carnival poster was mounted on the wall above Grace. AMAZING CYCLE SPECTACULAR! the poster read, above a stylized illustration of twin motorcycles passing in mid-air. STARRING BARTON AND JOHNNY BLAZE!

Mack knew only too well that the colorful poster was the very last to advertise that particular show. *Does Johnny keep these souvenirs around to remind him of happier days*, he wondered, *or does he just like to torture himself for some reason?*

There were lots of things Mack didn't understand about his employer. Johnny's obsession with metaphysics for instance. Stacks and stacks of books were piled up around Grace, helping to prop the decrepit

Harley up. Multiple translations of the Bible, the Koran, and the Bhagavad-Gita were mixed in with volumes on voodoo, spiritualism, witchcraft, astrology, exorcism, reincarnation, and other occult topics. Post-its flagged specific pages. Tarot cards were used as bookmarks. Pagan idols and crystal talismans gathered dust on a nearby shelf. Mack scanned the titles of some of the books. *The Necronomicon. The Book of the Damned. The Tragedie of Doctor Faustus. Visions of the Vishanti. The Satanic Bible. The Darkhold for Dummies. . . .*

He shook his head. What in creation did Johnny see in all this spooky gobbledygook? What exactly was he looking for? He nodded at the overflowing piles of hardcovers and paperbacks, which threatened to topple over at any minute. "See you finally found a use for your books."

Johnny refused to take the bait. He knew what Mack thought of his more eccentric reading matter. "You want some jellies?"

"No, I don't want any of your weird candy." He gave Johnny a solemn look. "I need to talk to you about something."

Sighing, Johnny slumped onto the couch. He rested his cowboy boots on a discarded engine block. His glass of jelly beans cradled in his lap, he waited expectantly as Mack sat down on an overstuffed easy chair across from him. The mechanic had to move a tire iron off the seat before he could sit down. "About what?" Johnny asked. He didn't sound too enthusiastic about this chat.

Perhaps he already suspected what was on his friend's mind.

Mack gestured toward the circus poster up on the wall. "How you're jumping on the anniversary of your father's accident." It had been nearly fifteen years since Barton Blaze had died out by Abilene. "The jump's impossible. You don't need to do it over flaming cars, too." Memories of tonight's near-fatal crash flashed through Mack's mind. "What are you trying to prove?"

"That it's me," Johnny said.

Mack didn't get it. "That it's you . . . ?"

"Riding the bike," Johnny stated cryptically.

"Who else would it be?" Mack threw up his hands in frustration. What the hell was Johnny talking about? "J. B., you know what? You're freaking me out here." He pointed at the heaping piles of occult texts. "You gotta stop reading all this . . . this exponential, comparative religiosity crap."

Johnny acted like he hadn't heard a word Mack was saying. His mind was clearly elsewhere. "Mack, do you believe people get second chances?"

"What?" He had no idea where Johnny was going with this.

"If someone makes a mistake," he said, his tone deadly serious, "a bad mistake, do you think they should have to pay for it every day for the rest of their life?"

Mack glanced again at the old carnival poster. "Are you talking about your dad?"

"Not exactly," Johnny said vaguely. Seeing the

mechanic's baffled expression, he offered something more by way of an explanation. "I'm just looking for a sign."

"A sign?" Mack echoed.

"That I'm alive."

Mack mulled that over. He felt like he was getting tantalizingly close to whatever was troubling his friend, but he couldn't quite fit the pieces together. "Johnny, what happened way back when wasn't your fault." As far as Mack knew, Barton Blaze had just pushed his luck one time too many. It was a tragedy, but those were the breaks. Johnny's dad had risked his life on a daily basis. One day the odds caught up with him; that was all. "You know that, right?"

Johnny didn't answer. His face shut down as he withdrew into some private purgatory deep inside him. Mack knew that he wouldn't be getting any more out of his friend tonight. He stood up to go.

"At least tell me you'll think about taking the cars out."

Johnny nodded absently, lost in his own melancholy musings. His haunted eyes stared blankly into his own lost soul. "I'll think about it."

Mack realized that was the best he could hope for, although he had few illusions that he had made any serious dent in Johnny's determination to proceed with the big anniversary stunt as planned. Times like this, he wished people were as easy to fix as a broken-down bike. Sadly, there was nothing in his toolbox that could straighten out whatever was damaged inside Johnny Blaze. *I don't think they make a socket wrench for a guilty conscience.*

Shaking his head, he exited the loft.

Johnny sat alone upon the couch, with only his books and Grace to keep him company.

The Broken Spoke Saloon was located on the outskirts of town. Raucous music and laughter escaped the open windows and graffiti-covered walls of the dingy biker bar. It was nearly one in the morning, but the party was still going strong. Earl "Big Daddy" Dawson leaned his considerable bulk up against the front of the building as he took a break from the drunken revelry to get a little fresh air. Rows of choppers were lined up on the pavement outside the bar. Broken glass, beer cans, and cigarette butts littered the front porch and parking lot. Cracked paint peeled off the front porch. A red neon sign flickered erratically. Wooden shutters guarded the windows. Heavy gray clouds threatened to rain at any moment.

A slim blonde waitress, whose jaded expression testified that she'd been around the block a few hundred times, stepped out of the bar. A white Daytona tank top and low-rise bluejeans exposed her pierced navel. A thorny rose was tattooed on her bare left shoulder. A cheap turquoise bracelet jangled on one arm. She handed a fresh bottle of beer to Big Daddy. "Here you go."

"Took you long enough," he grumbled.

Carrie Schultz took his bluster in stride, even though

Dawson was an intimidating figure by most anyone's standards. A permanent scowl was etched into his broad, wind-burned face. He had a bald dome and an unkempt beard. Prison tattoos inked up his beefy arms and thick neck. An iron cross rested upon his hairy chest. A Nazi dagger was tucked into his belt. The patches on his leather vest identified him as a full member of the "Fallen Angels," one of the Southwest's most notorious biker gangs. The Angels were heavily into drugs, extortion, sexual assault, and murder for hire. They made the infamous Mongols look like choirboys in comparison.

What's an Angel gotta do to get some decent service around here? he thought irritably. If it wasn't so damn hot, he'd teach Carrie not to keep a thirsty man waiting. A couple of black eyes would get the lead out of her butt, he bet. *Serve her right, too.*

An impatient voice called out to the waitress from inside the bar, so she left Earl alone on the porch. He took a swig from his beer, then peered at the bottle in surprise. Right before his puzzled eyes, the longneck bottle was icing up on the outside. *What the hell?* he thought, more irked than amazed by this seeming miracle. It was at least ninety-five degrees outside.

He started to yell for the waitress again, intending to demand an explanation for the frosty anomaly, but was distracted by something else.

Now what? he thought crankily.

A figure was approaching from the darkness. Moving

at a deliberate pace, he walked out of the desert toward the Broken Spoke. The neon lights of the bar revealed a slender young man with a pale complexion. He was elegantly—and inappropriately—dressed in a stylish black suit, complete with a dark silk shirt and velvet waistcoat. Slick black hair was tucked neatly in place. Dark smudges accented his piercing black eyes. The tails of his long black coat folded behind him like a raven's wings. His lean shadow stretched out upon the dusty road behind him.

Dawson took him for one of those fancy-pants Goth types.

The biker put the ice-cold bottle down on a window sill and rose menacingly to his full height. He loomed before the bar's open front door, his brawny arms crossed atop his barrel chest.

"I think you must be lost, boy."

Ignoring Big Daddy, the youth closed his eyes and concentrated, as if intent on locating something with his remaining senses. Dawson couldn't help noticing that the ordinary sounds of the desert at night—the flutter of wings, the yip of coyotes, the rattle of a disturbed serpent—had abruptly fallen silent. *What's that all about?*

The youth opened his eyes. A feral smile suggested that his efforts had been amply rewarded. Heedless of the hulking biker in his path, he stepped briskly toward the bar, although what he expected to find inside, aside from a well-deserved beating, was anybody's guess.

Dawson glowered at the younger man. "You deaf or something?"

The youth headed straight for the door. Earl didn't budge. The intruder's eyes met Dawson's, as if noticing him for the first time. Not a flicker of apprehension appeared upon the youth's delicate, epicene features. He met Big Daddy's belligerent stare with unruffled calm, which only pissed off the biker more. Dawson jabbed a meaty finger into the youth's chest.

"Angels only in there, boy."

The youth's smile widened. "Really?" His soft voice had a cultured air that seemed incongruous at the seamy biker bar.

Big Daddy clenched his fists. "You got a problem with that?"

"As a matter of fact . . ."

The youth jabbed his own finger into Earl—and it *sank* right into the biker's chest. Dawson stiffened in shock, his mouth opening wide in a silent scream, as a strange ectoplasmic substance flowed into his body, turning his bloodshot eyes and skin a deep shade of midnight blue. The poisonous ichor spread outward from the biker's wicked heart, freezing him in place as this toxin—this *necroplasm*—infiltrated every cell of his body, flowing into his extremities. His fear-stricken eyes stared into those of the youth, which were aglow with demonic energy, as though he was literally feeding on Dawson's mounting pain and horror. The biker's eyes glazed over. His flesh sagged beneath his skin, which cracked open above his withered muscles and tendons. Rotting from the inside out, he collapsed onto the creaky wooden porch. His tongue turned black inside his gaping jaws before falling out entirely. Indigo eyes dissolved into pools of gelid muck. Faded tattoos peeled away from his desiccated bones. The man's riding leathers looked absurdly oversized upon the mummified blue corpse at the youth's feet.

". . . I do," Blackheart finished.

The party was over. Shriveled blue corpses were scattered throughout the squalid interior of the saloon. Poisoned bikers and their old ladies slumped over tables or lay sprawled upon the sawdust floor. Several of the mummies still clutched knives or chains, not that the weapons had done them any good. A burly blond biker, his skeletal fist wrapped around a cue, lay prone atop the green felt surface of the pool table. Spilled drinks pooled upon the floor, beside discarded dice and drug paraphernalia. Several chairs and tables were overturned. The jukebox had gone mute. A dartboard hung upon one wall, a game interrupted in progress. A ceiling fan spun steadily, doing little to relieve the stuffy atmosphere, which reeked of tobacco, alcohol, marijuana, and just the slightest hit of brimstone. Everyone present bore the telltale blue sheen of the necroplasm. Within minutes, the rowdy bar had become a morgue. Not a soul appeared to have been spared.

Frightened out of her wits, Carrie cowered behind

the bar. Mascara streaked her face as she bit down on her lower lip in order to keep from screaming and/or sobbing. She huddled beneath the counter, afraid to make a peep, or even breathe, for fear of giving away her hiding place. The only survivor of the blue-tinged nightmare that had consumed her friends and coworkers, she clung to the desperate hope that she might live to see the dawn.

If she could, she would have contracted herself into a microscopic speck if that was what it took to stay out of sight from the . . . creature . . . who had invaded the Broken Spoke. She crossed herself instinctively.

It had all happened so fast. One minute it was just another rowdy night at the saloon. The Angels had drunk and drugged and gambled and argued while plotting their next big road trip and criminal enterprise. Dirty jokes had elicited guffaws and groans. A couple of near-fights had broken out, mostly over that slut Marlene. Bikes and gear were bought and sold, mostly depending on who had some ready cash this week, and who was hard-up for bail money. A cloud of second-hand smoke, mixed with a tinge of pot, bought everyone in the bar a one-way trip to the cancer ward, provided any of them lived that long. Carrie had spent most of her time pouring beer and whiskey down the throats of thirsty bikers when she wasn't dodging horny desperadoes who wanted to play grab-ass every time she came within arm's reach. *Sorry, boys,* she'd thought. *That don't come free.* The jukebox had blared nonstop, loud enough to make your ears bleed. Massive quantities of coke and meth had fueled the hardcore partying.

The usual.

Then in came this skinny dude with his fancy duds and a face paler than Michael Jackson's. Carrie had figured he was dead meat the minute she laid eyes on him; at the very least he was cruising for a serious bruising. But the creep didn't even seem to realize that he was in the wrong place; instead he had just sidled up to the bar and started looking around like he owned the joint. Wild Bill had been the first to get in his face. No surprise there, Bill never missed a chance to kick butt. That's why he had all those assault charges pending.

And why he was the first to die.

Carrie had never seen anything like it. Bill never saw it coming. The creepy Goth guy just reached out and touched Bill and the hardcore biker suddenly turned all blue and disgusting. He was dead before any of his brother Angels even realized what was happening.

But after Bill hit the floor, all hell broke loose. Every Angel in the place came at the intruder, swinging chains and knives, brass knuckles and fists. It didn't do any good, though. The white-faced demon just strolled through the bar, killing people left and right, without even breaking a sweat. He broke Axel's neck with his bare hands, and ripped Bulldog's heart from his chest, but mostly he just poisoned people with his toxic fingertips. The same blue death that killed Bill also sucked the life from many others the demon got hold off.

Pretty soon, people were screaming and running for the exits. But the stranger waved his hand and every door slammed shut, refusing to budge. Hardened bikers, real one-percenters, were crying like babies, afraid they were going to Hell. The other waitresses started dying too. Marlene pleaded with for her life, like the tramp she was, but it didn't save her. No one was spared, not the Angels, not the staff, no one.

Until only Carrie was left.

Please, God, she prayed, *don't let this devil claim my soul.* She had led a wild and sinful life, she knew, filled with drugs and booze and far too many men. Her rebellious ways had broken her poor mother's heart and scandalized the nuns who had tried so hard to teach her right from wrong. To be honest, shocking the stern sisters had been half the fun at first, before the heavy-duty partying had become the only life she knew. She'd had a child once, a little boy, but she had dumped the baby on her mother the first chance she'd got. Little Mickey was five now. Carrie couldn't remember the last time she'd spoken with him. Maybe his birthday, or the one before that?

But I can change, she insisted, frantically bargaining with God. *Just let me get through tonight and I promise I will turn my life around. I'll go back to church. I'll get off the dope. I'll go back to school. Get a decent job.* She closed her eyes and fervently pleaded for Heaven's mercy. *Rescue me from this monster, and I swear I'll never speak to another biker for as long as I live!*

For a moment, it appeared her prayers had been answered. Listening intently, she heard footsteps leaving the tavern. The front door slammed shut on its hinges. Silence fell over the murdered saloon. Holding her breath, she heard only the steady dripping from the leaky roof. *I always told Duke to fix that,* she thought irrationally. The tavern's owner was now one of the cobalt-colored corpses slumped over the bar.

Carrie hesitated, not quite trusting her good fortune. She was tempted to bolt for the back door right away, then put as many miles as possible between herself and the Broken Spoke, but caution kept her hiding beneath the bar, just to be safe. She was no fool; years tending to ex-cons and other outlaws had taught how to look out for herself in tough situations. She wasn't going to take any stupid chances.

Let's make sure he's really gone, she decided. *Give him plenty of time to leave this place behind.*

She counted slowly to one hundred, then counted again. Anxious minutes dragged out endlessly as her cramped leg muscles shrieked in protest. Tequila dripped over the edge of the counter above her, pooling on the floor. Carrie stayed put, trying unsuccessfully to recall all the words to the Lord's Prayer, until she felt confidant that the demonic killer *had* to be far away by now. Taking a deep breath, she crawled out from beneath the bar and rose unsteadily to her feet.

Blackheart was waiting for her.

Carrie opened her mouth to scream, but the black-garbed youth was too quick for her. Clamping a hand over her mouth, he lunged forward and pulled her across the counter. Spilled tequila soaked through the front of her tank top. Her heart pounded like a jack-rabbit's. Despite his slight appearance, the youth was amazingly strong. Carrie could no more break free from his grip than she could have snapped apart a pair of titanium handcuffs. She could only squirm helplessly in the intruder's grasp. A muffled shriek disappeared into Blackheart's palm, which smelled faintly of sulfur.

"I knew you were here," he said calmly. "I could feel your fear." His eerie yellow eyes locked onto hers and set her teeth chattering. The greater her fear, the more avidly his eyes gleamed, as though they were soaking up every last ounce of her terror. "You are going to die now. I am going to devour your soul." He gave her a smile that was not at all comforting. "It will feel worse than you can possibly imagine."

Sheer, unrelenting panic threatened to drive her insane. She screamed hysterically into her captor's hand. *Mickey!* she thought in anguish, picturing her child's cherubic face. Years of guilt tore at her heart. *I should have been there for you!* What if she never had a chance to make things right?

"Please . . . don't kill me," Carrie sobbed. "I have a son . . . a five-year-old son . . ."

Blackheart nodded in approval. "You will never see

him again." His victim whimpered in agony. "Does that hurt you?" He seemed fascinated by her reaction. "I want you to think of that. Keep thinking of it . . . forever."

He took his hand away from her mouth.

Carrie screamed until there was nothing left of her. A withered blue skeleton dropped to the floor.

Blackheart felt remarkably refreshed.

"Angels tossed from Heaven, forced to live on Earth," he observed. He eyed the shabby tavern with disdain. Neon signs and stolen license plates were nailed to the rough wooden walls. A mounted boar head glared down from above the jukebox. A stuffed coyote perched upon a shelf. Profanities were scrawled on every available surface. Blackheart turned up his nose at the general squalor and bad taste of the furnishings. "And this is the spot you choose?"

He smirked at the tavern's mummified bartender. Rigor mortis held the dead man upright behind the bar, paralyzed in the act of pouring tequila into a dirty cup. The liquor had poured into an overflowing glass mug, the excess tequila spilling over the top of the cup onto the cigarette-burned surface of the counter. Shredded military fatigues clothed the cobalt-colored corpse. A half-empty bowl of beer nuts waited to be refilled.

"But you have managed to remain hidden," he conceded. "Impressive."

He strolled across the violated tavern, stepping lightly over indigo bodies. The looming summer storm finally hit outside and heavy rain pelted the tin roof overhead. Water dripped from a leak in the ceiling, hitting the counter with a staccato rhythm that reminded Blackheart of the infamous Chinese Water Torture. *One of the mortals' better ideas*, he recalled nostalgically. *Although it works even better with demon's bile.*

"Living like scavengers off the scraps humans cast aside, like carrion waiting to feed." His gaze swept the seemingly lifeless tavern. The mottled blue corpses did not respond, nor did he expect them to. "Show yourselves."

An empty pair of cowboy boots rested atop a filthy table. A black centipede crawled up onto the tabletop, followed by animated clumps of cracked earth and clay that had been tracked onto the floor by the bar's dead patrons. A thick column of dirt and sawdust snaked up onto a chair, congealing into the figure of man.

Within seconds, a thuggish young man materialized upon the chair. He leaned back, keeping the formerly empty boots on the table. A brown snakeskin coat was draped over his bare chest. His close-cropped hair was the color of red clay. Bulging veins streaked his brow. Yellow eyes gleamed with malice. A heavy layer of grime appeared to cover the man's face and garments, until a closer look revealed that the pockmarked flesh was literally composed of dirt, sawdust, and wriggling insects.

"Gressil," Blackheart addressed the newcomer.

The metronomic beat of the falling rain was joined by the sound of a dirty puddle spreading across the floor. The turbid water flowed upward and took the shape of a lanky figure leaning against a window. His vulpine face was as white as a drowned man's. Long, stringy hair clung damply to his narrow skull. His water-logged duster was green as mildew. Azure eyes peered out from behind wet strands of hair. He tilted back his head, letting the rain splash against his face like a barroom baptism. The water did not just run down his face; his face *was* water. He wiped a runny eye off his fluid cheek.

"Wallow," Blackheart said.

A sudden breeze rattled the wooden shutters as it blew into the room. The foul wind carried a cloud of airborne dirt and gravel, along with the stench of an open sewer. The swirling grime assumed the form of a pale, bearded man with a thick mane of matted black hair. A perpetual gale seemed to rustle his greasy dreadlocks and fur-trimmed leather coat. His sneering face fluttered in the breeze. He casually lit a cigarette before smirking at Blackheart. The smoke from the cigarette formed a miniature whirlwind.

"Abigor," Blackheart greeted him. He contemplated the uncanny trio before him. These were the Hidden, demonic elementals that dwelt unseen upon the mortal plane. Capable of blending with the material substance of the world, they hid easily from the pathetic senses of the humans. As far as the mortals were concerned, the Hidden could be almost anywhere.

Even a sleazy biker bar.

"The last of the Fallen Angels." He grinned at the demons. "Where you been hiding, boys?"

The three elementals exchanged nervous looks among themselves.

"Why did you summon us here?" Abigor whispered. "We've stayed hidden all these years. If Mephistopheles should find us . . ."

"Mephistopheles is dead," Blackheart declared, cutting him off. The demons stared at him in disbelief. "He just doesn't know it yet."

"What do you want from us?" Gressil asked suspiciously. His raspy voice sounded like he was gargling with rocks.

"I've come to start a New Hell on Earth," Blackheart informed them. "You can either join me . . ." He gestured toward the abundant corpses. "Or you can join them."

Understanding dawned in the demons' eyes. Wallow stepped forward from his window sill. "You've come to start the War."

"But you have no soldiers," Abigor protested. "No army."

"I'll be my *own* army," Blackheart said, "once I have the Contract of San Venganza."

The demons' eyes widened in surprise, as word of the legend met their ears. "The Contract of a Thousand Souls," Wallow gurgled in awe.

Blackheart nodded. "The souls have grown more powerful with time. In Hell, they'd tip the balance in

Mephistopheles's favor. But here on Earth, in my hands, they'll become more powerful than even he could ever imagine."

"But the Contract was lost," Gressil recalled.

Blackheart shook his head. "Not lost. Stolen. Legend says it was hidden in a graveyard not far from here. You're going to help me find it." He beamed in anticipation. "And then we'll take this world . . . one city at a time."

The elementals grinned back at him, the notion obviously appealing to them. But before they could reply, a booming voice called angrily from outside the saloon:

"BLACKHEART!"

Naturally, Blackheart thought, undisturbed by the interruption. He had been expecting this.

Heeding the call, Blackheart burst through the tavern's swinging doors and strode confidently onto the porch outside. A wicked smile crept across his face as he spotted a familiar figure waiting for him beyond the parked motorcycles.

The golden-haired old man leaned upon his distinctive silver cane, with a crystal skull grinning atop it. The man's long black coat stretched from his neck down to his ankles. Black eyes fixed on the younger man, who appeared to be alone upon the porch. So far, the Hidden were living up to their name.

"Hello, *Father*," Blackheart said coldly.

Mephistopheles was in no mood for pleasantries. "How dare you defy me?"

89

"It's my time now, old man." In truth, Blackheart had been looking forward to this inevitable encounter. He beckoned silently to his allies, who remained concealed from view.

"*I decide your time!*" the Devil roared furiously. His anger momentarily shredded his mortal facade, revealing his true features. Demonic black eyes and shriveled blue skin were briefly exposed.

"Not anymore," Blackheart declared. At his command, the Hidden materialized around his father. They gnashed their fangs as they circled Mephistopheles like a pack of hungry jackals. "Did you really think I was going to wait around for your *permission?*"

The Devil ignored the fallen angels surrounding him. That he was outnumbered four to one did not seem to trouble him. "You violate the Order by coming here."

"What 'Order'?" Blackheart asked incredulously. "Take a look around. You're playing by the rules of a forgotten game. Nobody cares what you do. Even God's lost interest."

Mephistopheles limped toward his son. The neon lights of the bar dimmed at his approach. "I've worked too long and too hard. Your time will come," he promised. "But not now."

"You think I want to rule your obsolete Hell. *Please.*" He sighed theatrically. "I **w**as meant for better things than that."

The Devil's expression darkened. "You will suffer for this. . . ."

"The only thing I'm suffering from is you." Blackheart couldn't resist the temptation to bait the old man. Emboldened by their leader's show of defiance, the Hidden cackled like hyenas. "We both know you can't harm me here. I'm not like you. I've never Fallen." He sneered at his father's skull-capped walking stick. "And I never will."

Mephistopheles glared at the youth. "I may not have power over you in this world," he warned ominously. "But my Ghost Rider does."

The Hidden cringed at the old man's words. Their mocking laughter was cut short. Blackheart was faintly disappointed by his minions' weak nerves, but no matter. He did not fear so feeble a threat.

"Of course. The Ghost Rider. Your *favorite* creation." Blackheart's eyes glowed crimson as a new flavor of resentment entered his voice. "The power of Hellfire *wasted* on one pathetic human after another! If you had trusted in me, if you had given me what was rightfully mine . . ."

"It's too late for that now," the Devil interrupted him. He dismissed Blackheart's jealousy with a wave of his hand. "Run along home now, son."

His father's arrogance infuriated Blackheart. Mephistopheles's best days were behind him. Why couldn't he see that?

"Send your Ghost Rider," he challenged his satanic sire. "I'll bury him just like I'll bury you, Father."

Mephistopheles glowered back at him. Thunder

boomed in the distance as, scowling, the Devil dissolved into the darkness. The neon lights flickered back on.

Blackheart smirked at his father's abrupt departure. No doubt the old man's pride would not allow him to concede defeat. *Well*, he thought, *Pride goeth before a fall.*

As his father of all people should know.

His eyes narrowed into angry slits as he gathered his companions around him. Blackheart stepped down from the porch and turned his gaze toward the horizon, where the bright city lights could be seen from miles away. It was time to get back down to business.

"Let's go to town," he said.

6

"BLAZE! BLAZE! BLAZE!"

The thunderous chanting penetrated the inner walls of Texas Stadium, reaching the private locker room where Johnny prepared for his much-hyped "Touchdown Jump." Karen Carpenter's soulful cover of "Superstar" played softly over the sound system as he zipped himself into a brand-new red-and-white riding suit. The mellow music helped to soothe his troubled soul. A flame-detailed crash helmet rested on a bench behind him.

He was almost ready.

Despite the excitement of the crowd, Johnny's own mood was subdued. He stared solemnly into the mirror over a sink. Haunted eyes, looking even more apathetic than usual, gazed back at him. It was fifteen years to the day since his father died. Johnny couldn't help wondering if this was also the day that he pushed his own luck too far. The day he *didn't* walk away.

Would that be the stranger's idea of joke? It had been nearly two decades since he had last seen the stranger, at that lonely crossroads outside of Sweetwater. Although he had promised to return someday, he had left Johnny alone so far. Johnny realized with a start that he had now spent nearly half his life dreading the inevitable day when the stranger came back into his life, to claim his half of the Faustian bargain they had struck so long ago. Fifteen wasted years . . . with only the dubious consolations of celebrity to occupy his time.

No wonder he wasn't afraid to die. At least the waiting would be over.

"J.B.?"

Mack's reflection appeared from behind in the mirror. He fidgeted in the doorway leading out of the locker room, then opened his mouth to speak.

"Shhh," Johnny said, holding a finger to his lips. "You're stepping on Karen." He waited for the last few bars of "Superstar" to play out before looking back over his shoulder at his friend. "What was it you were going to say?"

Looking uncomfortable, Mack worked up his nerve to speak. "Just . . . you don't have to go through with this, you know?"

Was that what Mack was worrying about? Johnny didn't bother to answer. Mack always fretted before a big stunt. Sometime he thought the mechanic would be happier working for someone who didn't risk his life for a living.

"This suit fit alright?" Johnny asked, changing the

subject. "It feels a little loose. I like a nice tight fit in the back."

Mack's shoulders slumped in resignation. "No. It's good."

The poor guy looked so miserable Johnny figured he had to say something to boost his morale. "You can't live in fear," he reminded Mack.

If you can call this living . . .

"BLAZE! BLAZE!"

It was almost time to answer the crowd's demand. Cradling his helmet under his arm, Johnny let Mack guide him through the concrete maze outside the locker room. The bare walls were painted an institutional shade of white. Stadium personnel and security offered them greetings and good luck as they made their way from the dressing rooms. Johnny nodded politely at the grinning well-wishers, but resisted getting drawn into any long conversations. He had over sixty-five thousand fans waiting for him.

"We're up ahead and to the right," Mack explained.

Johnny took his word for it. After years on the road, all these backstage areas looked the same to him. He trusted Mack to tell them apart.

A woman in a crisp blue blazer fell in beside them. "Hi. Amy Page. Event publicity." A plastic name badge confirmed her I.D. "I was wondering if Mr. Blaze had time for a quick interview."

Mack gave her an incredulous look. "Lady, I don't

know how long you've been doing your job, but Johnny don't do no interviews."

"Not even for an old friend?" a husky voice intruded.

Johnny stopped dead in his tracks. His brain, which had barely registered the young publicist's presence, suddenly snapped to attention. Even though it had been fifteen years since he last heard that voice, he recognized it at once.

Roxanne.

She stood at the far end of the corridor, silhouetted by the stadium lights outside. A spotless white dress flattered her voluptuous figure, which had filled out nicely since her teenage years. Her lustrous auburn hair was elegantly coiffed. Cool brown eyes flashed with strength and confidence. Time had been more than kind to her; maturity had only enhanced her natural beauty and magnetism. No longer a coltish adolescent, she was now a woman to be reckoned with.

A microphone resided in her right hand. Her cameraman, a skinny white dude in a baseball cap, hovered behind her, rendered all but invisible by her radiance. Johnny was well aware, of course, that Roxanne had become a top cable news reporter. Late at night, when nobody else was around, he had spent many long insomniac hours watching her on TV. He had even Googled her a couple of times. But none of that had prepared him for the shock of unexpectedly finding her right in front of him after all these years. *All the stadiums in all the world,* he thought, *and she has to walk into this one.*

Distracted, Mack didn't pick up on Johnny's stunned reaction. "Look, miss," he began, "no offense, but—"

"I'll do it," Johnny said impulsively.

Mack stared at Johnny in disbelief. He couldn't have looked more surprised if Johnny had suddenly traded in his Harleys for a Prius.

Seizing the opportunity, the cameraman hastily got into position. He didn't need to tell Johnny not to look directly into the camera; the world-famous daredevil couldn't take his eyes off Roxanne. An awkward moment ensued as Johnny wondered what he could possibly say to her after so many years. The last time he'd seen Roxanne Simpson in the flesh, she had been a shrinking figure in Grace's rear-view mirror.

She looked him over coolly, her immaculately composed face betraying no hint of whatever she might be feeling at the moment. Had she ever forgiven him for abandoning her without explanation the day his father died?

How could she?

"Oh, you're looking at the suit," he said nervously. He suddenly felt extremely self-conscious. "I know it looks silly, but the fans like it so I keep on wearing it."

Roxanne nodded, her expression neutral.

She wasn't making this easy on him. Why should she?

The cameraman signaled that he was ready. "Okay, in five, four . . ."

"How's your dad?" Johnny blurted.

"One!"

Roxanne instantly went into action. A camera-ready smile appeared on her face.

"Johnny Blaze, thank you for talking to us before your big jump." She was all business, professional. "No one has ever attempted such a distance before. Three hundred feet from field goal to field goal." She thrust the mike toward him. "What's going through your mind right now?"

Not the jump, that was for sure.

"You look really good," he said. "You know, I've seen you on TV. I watch a lot of TV and you do a really great job. Like an angel sent down from heaven. With a microphone."

Roxanne blinked, but managed to maintain her impartial demeanor. She didn't even blush. "Johnny, what drives someone to risk their life for entertainment?"

"I heard you got married?" He had stopped Googling her after seeing an item about her engagement in the Lifestyles section of a Dallas newspaper. It had seemed wrong somehow.

"No, that didn't happen," she murmured, *sotto voce*. Raising her voice, she turned to face the camera. "Most of the time, the press focuses on the crashes, the broken bones, the tangible costs of what you do." She closed in on Johnny, pushing him to open up. "But are there other costs?"

The question struck home, perhaps even more than she intended. Once again, Johnny remembered a younger Roxanne standing forlorn upon Crowley Hill, a confused and heartbroken expression upon her lovely face. He hesitated before answering, letting the silence stretch out a beat too long.

"Uh . . . yeah."

Roxanne took the microphone back, looking a bit flummoxed. She gazed at Johnny with a slightly more vulnerable expression, like she both wanted and didn't want to know what he meant. He thought he saw a hint of the sixteen-year-old girl he had once held in his arms. Out of the corner of her eye, she spotted Mack tapping his watch.

"Okay, well . . ." It took her a moment to segue back into reporter mode. "Thank you for this . . . revealing . . . peek into the life of Johnny Blaze." She turned back to the camera with an almost palpable look of relief. "I'm Roxanne Simpson, live at Texas Stadium."

The cameraman signaled that he had the sign-off in the can. He started to pack up his gear. Johnny spoke up quickly, before she could get away.

"You're going to stay for the jump, right?"

Roxanne lowered her microphone. She shook her head. "We've got to get back. Besides, I never liked watching you jump."

That's not how I remember it. He vividly recalled her younger self cheering him on from the front row of the circus bleachers.

But a lot had changed since then.

"It was great seeing you, Johnny," she said politely.

Spinning around on her heels, she walked out the door before he could even say good-bye. *Talk about karma coming back to bite you. I had that coming.* He watched her disappear out the exit.

Mack finally caught on. "I'm going to go out on a limb and say you two have some kind of history."

"That was it, Mack," Johnny said in a hushed tone. "The sign."

Maybe there was such a thing a second chance after all? For the first time in years, he found himself excited about the future. Maybe the Devil didn't really own his soul. Perhaps he wasn't cursed after all. Suddenly, he was eager to find out.

Assuming he survived the next thirty minutes . . .

Texas Stadium, ordinarily the home of the Dallas Cowboys, had been done up proper for Johnny Blaze's "Touchdown Jump." Colored banners, emblazoned with bright red cartoon flames, festooned the bleachers, which were packed to capacity. Today's event had been sold out for weeks, with scalpers charging obscene fees for even the nosebleed seats. The domed ceiling covered the bleachers, but not the field itself. A large rectangular opening let in the bright afternoon sunshine. Texans liked to joke that the hole in the ceiling was there so that "God can watch His team."

Special modifications had been made for the cycle show. An insanely vertical ski ramp ran from the top of the stadium and down through the goal posts, with the landing ramp in the *other* end zone one hundred yards away. Jumbotron TV screens flanked the cherry-red take-off ramp. A lengthy expanse of green AstroTurf stretched between the towering yellow goal posts. The rhythmic chanting of the audience exploded into a deafening roar as Johnny appeared at the top of the ramp. The humongous TV screens treated the fans to a close-up of the celebrated daredevil atop his bike.

Johnny pumped his fists and both goal posts burst into flame.

The crowd somehow managed to cheer even louder.

Here we go again, Mack thought. He avoided looking down the vertigo-inducing ski ramp as he handed Johnny his crash helmet. Instead he gazed out across the intimidating length of the football field below. The other ramp seemed impossibly far away. Acid ate away at the pit of his stomach. He would have killed for a Tums.

"Thank God you listened to me and took out the cars," Mack said, raising his voice to be heard over the roar of the crowd. "That would have been suicide. Now if you come up short, you'll just land on some nice, soft AstroTurf." A shadow passed over his face and he looked up in confusion. "Huh?"

To his dumbfounded amazement, a squadron of six black Lynx helicopters descended through the rectangular gap in the ceiling. Their spinning rotors whipped up the air inside the arena as they touched down on the football field, lining up in a row between the flaming goal posts. Their blades kept on spinning.

Slack-jawed and speechless, Mack looked to Johnny for an explanation.

Johnny shrugged his shoulders.

"I took out the cars."

The parking lot was packed. Roxanne and her cameraman, Stuart, had to trek through acres of parked vehicles before they reached their navy-blue news van. The hot sun beat down on them, turning the pavement into a frying pan. Roxanne sweated beneath her professional attire—the crisp white dress began to wilt.

The heat wasn't the only thing bothering her. Even though she had prepared herself emotionally for her reunion with Johnny, the damn rider had gotten under her skin anyway. The adoring look in his eyes, the loneliness in his voice, had touched something she had thought dead and buried for years now. The sweet fragrance of Texas bluebonnets, spread out across a grassy hillside, surfaced from her memory. She remembered holding tightly onto Johnny's waist as she rode behind him on his father's powerful Harley-Davidson. There was a time when she would have given anything for that ride not to end, back when their future had seemed as wide-open as the endless highway stretched out before them.

Once upon a time, she had thought Johnny felt the same way.

Get over it, she told herself. *That was a long time ago. We're not the same people anymore.*

Stuart opened up the van and started stowing away his gear. From where she was standing, he seemed to be taking his own sweet time about it. She tapped her foot impatiently against the hot blacktop.

"Can we get out of here already?"

The helicopters' blades whirred like giant buzzsaws. Mack couldn't believe his eyes. "You replaced the cars with *helicopters?*" he shouted, finding his voice. "So if you come up short you'll be sliced and diced in a human food processor?!"

Of all the crazy, suicidal stunts . . . !

"Take it easy," Johnny said.

Was he freaking serious? Mack threw up his hands. "Why didn't you tell me about this?"

"Because you would have thrown a fit," Johnny explained. Mack tried to figure out how Johnny could have possibly arranged all this behind his back.

"Yeah, I'm funny that way! Human sacrifices make me uncomfortable!" Mack forced himself not to blow his top. He searched his friend's face, genuinely trying to understand. "Why, Johnny?"

Johnny smiled, a sad look on his face. "My dad thought it would be cool."

His dad who died fifteen years ago today. Now

that he thought of it, Mack dimly remembered Johnny telling him something about Barton Blaze's dream stunt, the one he'd had in mind right before crashing his bike for the last time. Mack slowly grasped that this was Johnny's way of honoring his father's memory.

Hell. How could he argue with that?

The two men stared down at the sleek black copters. They looked infinitely snazzier than any row of burning trucks ever had. Damn, but it was hard to fault the showmanship involved.

"He was right," Mack admitted. Taking a deep breath to steady his nerves, he tried to adjust to a whole new game plan. "Okay, now remember to hit your NOS mid-way through the take-off ramp. Don't wait for lift-off or you're gonna . . ." Johnny was staring off into space, barely listening to him. "Hey, where's your head at?"

Johnny remained lost in thought, a dreamy expression upon his face. "I should have stopped her."

Her? Mack wondered briefly who Johnny could possibly have his head in the clouds over at such a time, then realized who he had to be talking about. *That smokin' reporter babe. The one he knew from before.*

"Well, I'll be damned," he said, chuckling to himself. In all the years Mack had known him, Johnny had never fallen hard for any chick, despite all the grease groupies throwing themselves at him. There were times Mack had wondered whether his friend had antifreeze in his veins and *cojones*. "Looks like you're flesh and blood after all."

The van's air-conditioning was a blessed relief after the heat of the parking lot. Roxanne settled into the passenger's seat while Stuart took the wheel. She knew she should be thinking about her deadlines, but instead she kept replaying her interview with Johnny in her mind. *I'll have to edit out some of the mushier parts*, she realized. *Like that bit where he compared me to an angel.*

What was he thinking?

The van pulled out of the parking lot onto the freeway. Despite herself, she couldn't resist adjusting the rear-view mirror to watch the stadium recede into the distance. She wondered if Johnny had attempted that crazy jump yet, but was afraid to turn on the radio to find out. For all she knew, he was already dead—just like his dad.

Her fiddling with the mirror did not escape Stuart's notice. "Leave something behind?" he teased.

She silenced him with a look.

The crowd inside the stadium grew restless as the big moment approached. A pair of announcers shamelessly hyped the event over the arena's public address system.

"Blaze and Chief Mechanic Randall Mackenzie run one final check," the first announcer observed as over-sized images of the two men flashed upon the gigantic TV screens at both ends of the stadium. A brand-new

XR 750 replaced the one Johnny had trashed at the motorway.

"You can feel the tension all the way up here in the booth, Jim," his partner added. His hushed tone only made the occasion seem more dangerous. "These men know that the slightest error can cost Johnny Blaze his life."

At the top of the ramp, though, Johnny wasn't at all worried about that. His brain was elsewhere. "She's probably on the interstate by now," he commented to Mack.

"Johnny? Hello?" Mack waved a hand in front of Johnny's face. His boss's newfound preoccupation with that hot reporter *chica* could not have come at a worse time. As happy as Mack was that Johnny had finally succumbed to Cupid's arrow, there was still the little matter of a certain death-defying stunt. "Sixty-five thousand people came to see you jump." He checked to make sure Johnny's crash helmet was on securely. "You gotta focus, man!"

To his relief, a determined expression came over Johnny's face. He looked more focused—more motivated—than he had in years. For once, he seemed to truly care whether he lived or died.

"How much giggle gas did you put in the tanks?" he asked urgently.

"Enough to shame the space shuttle," Mack said, glad to see Johnny taking an interest in his own survival at last. Maybe that reporter was a good influence on him after all. "Why?"

Johnny just grinned and slapped down his face shield.

Gunning the engine, he whacked open the throttle and took off down the sickeningly steep ramp. Plumes of white smoke jetted from the 750's exhaust pipes.

The crowd leapt to its feet. This was what they had been waiting all day for.

"And here goes Blaze!" the announcer exclaimed.

Mack could barely watch. He squeezed his eyes shut as the spanking new stunt bike rocketed down the ramp and took off through the fiery uprights. Had Johnny fired off the nitrous oxide system in time? It was hard to tell, especially with your eyes closed.

"He's not going to make it," the uptight gearhead muttered, just like he always did whenever Johnny attempted a new stunt. Acid reflux climbed up his throat. "He's not going to make it. . . ."

He peeked between his fingers as Johnny soared above the whirring blades of the half-dozen helicopters. A collective gasp nearly sucked in all the air in the stadium. The smell of burning nitrous reached Mack's nostrils. Hitting the apogee of its airborne arc, the bike began to descend toward the distant landing ramp . . . with three more copters still to clear.

"He's not going to make it. . . ."

Mack was convinced that he had a closed-coffin funeral in his future.

Johnny cleared the final copter by less than a yard and, just barely, touched down on the sloping red ramp beneath another set of burning goal posts.

The cycle wobbled slightly on impact, but stayed upright. Johnny kept the bike under control as he cruised down the ramp.

"Blaze has done it!" the announcer shouted into his mike. Tens of thousands of cycle fans whooped and hollered and threw their souvenir programs into the air. Pandemonium broke out inside Texas Stadium. Fireworks on the field sprayed fountains of white sparks into the air. There hadn't been so much cheering and clapping beneath the open roof since the last time the Cowboys made it into the Super Bowl.

"Unbelievable!" the other announcer enthused. *"Absolutely incredible!"*

Relief flooded Mack's entire body. Beaming, he uncovered his eyes and hollered back at the stage crew behind him.

"I told you he'd make it!"

Straining his eyes, he watched Johnny slide to a stop at the opposite side of the stadium. The helicopters' rotors slowly stopped spinning. Johnny removed his helmet, revealing his disheveled black hair, and pumped his fist in the air. The Jumbotron screens revealed an uncharacteristic grin on the daredevil's face.

Mack felt his insides relax. He immediately wanted to send flowers to Roxanne Simpson.

"Johnny Blaze has set a new world—"

Then, to everyone's surprise, Johnny jammed his helmet back on and revved his engine again. Mack blinked in confusion as the bike sped toward the exit ramp behind the goal posts. He didn't know what was happening.

Neither did anyone else.

"Hey!" the startled announcer blurted. "Where's he going?"

7

THE NEWS VAN CRUISED EAST DOWN TX-183, HEADING for downtown Dallas. Suburban parks and developments rushed past their windows. Street signs pointed out the way to the University. Traffic wasn't too bad yet. Roxanne was glad they had left the stadium before the big rush after the event. She settled back into her seat.

"I'll say one thing," Stuart commented, breaking the silence. "The guy's got guts. The other night I was watching—"

Roxanne bristled. "Can we *please* stop talking about Johnny Blaze already?"

The cameraman glanced at the rear-view mirror. "That might be a little hard. . . ."

What's that supposed to mean? Peering back over her shoulder, Roxanne was shocked to see Johnny Blaze himself, zooming after them on his garish stunt cycle. He flashed his headlight to get her attention. Was the modified Harley even remotely street-legal? Johnny didn't seem to care. Switching lanes, he pulled alongside the van. He flipped up the visor on his crash helmet.

"I made it!" he shouted, grinning, his voice muffled by the window between them. The unmistakable roar of a V-Twin engine penetrated the van's front cabin. "I need to talk to you!"

Roxanne did a double-take, caught off-guard by Johnny's unexpected appearance. *All these years and he comes chasing after me now?* She rolled down her window.

"I need to talk to you!" he repeated.

This is insane. Biting down her lip, she struggled to maintain her composure as her past caught up with her at sixty miles per hour. The sound of the motorcycle's engine stirred her memory, throwing her back to her carnival days. Stuart helpfully slowed down.

"You want me to pull over?" he asked.

Hell, no! "Drive!" she ordered.

"Driving." Stuart stepped on the gas and she rolled her window back up, cutting off Johnny's fervent pleas. *I am not doing this right now,* she decided. Johnny had no right crashing back in her life like this, just when she thought she was over him. He'd had his chance fifteen years ago and he'd her left in the dust. *I don't owe him anything.*

Johnny dropped back behind the van, and, for a moment, she thought that he'd gotten the message. She breathed a sigh of relief, trying not to acknowledge a simultaneous twinge of disappointment. "Ahem," Stuart muttered, cocking his head to the left. Roxanne's eyes widened at the sight of Johnny coming up fast on the driver's side of the speeding van.

Apparently he wasn't giving up so easily.

Roxanne didn't know whether to be flattered or seriously pissed off.

Johnny pulled up alongside Stuart's window. The lanky cameraman gave her a helpless shrug, as though to ask what she expected him to do. Roxanne wished she knew.

All I wanted was an interview . . . right?

Determined not to look at Johnny, she fixed her gaze on the road ahead, only to experience a sudden surge of panic as she saw a eighty-ton semitrailer barreling straight toward him. Intent on getting through to her, Johnny seemed oblivious to the oncoming vehicle.

"Johnny, look out!"

He looked up in time to see the big rig rushing toward him. The bike burned rubber as it surged ahead and veered sharply to the right, barely missing the semi's front fender.

"Jesus!" Stuart yelped as the motorcycle screeched to a halt directly in front of the van.

The startled cameraman slammed on the brakes, throwing both him and Roxanne forward in their seats. A taut seat belt kept her from flying through the windshield, but she was too scared for Johnny to even notice the restraint. She held her breath as the speeding news van skidded to a halt only inches away from the stationary bike and rider. Horns honked and brakes squealed behind the van as their sudden stop set off a chain reaction all along the freeway. How they managed to avoid a multicar pileup she would never know. Beside her, Stuart slumped forward over the steering wheel, gasping. His narrow face was white as a sheet.

The color gradually returned to Roxanne's face as well. She took a second to thank every angel in heaven that Johnny had not been flattened beneath the van's wheels . . . then her temper got the better of her.

What the hell was he thinking, pulling a lunatic stunt like that? Has he lost his mind? She wouldn't be surprised to find out that every hair on her head had turned white. *How dare he scare me out of my wits like that?*

She threw open the van door and clambered down onto the asphalt. A chorus of angry voices and blaring car horns assailed her, but Roxanne was only interested in what one particular rider had to say. She marched toward Johnny, as he walked his bike to the side of the road. Waving apologetically back at the drivers behind him, Stuart obligingly pulled the van onto the shoulder, too.

"You almost got yourself killed!" she railed at Johnny. Her poised, professional manner had gone bye-bye. "What are you doing?"

Johnny sat meekly astride his bike. "I wanted to talk." He took off his helmet and hung it on the handlebars in front of him. "I haven't seen you in so long and then, blam, here you are and . . ."

"This is crazy!" she interrupted him. "You're crazy."

She threw her hands up in the air. She didn't know whether to punch him or have him committed. "I've got a piece to edit. I don't have time for this, Johnny."

She spun around and stomped back toward the van, leaving him behind for the second time this afternoon. *Maybe this time it will take.*

"You could have said 'no,' " he called after her. She paused and looked back at him with a scowl. A skeptical eyebrow arched. "When they asked you to interview me. You could have said 'no.' "

Actually, the interview had been her idea, but she didn't feel like mentioning that now. She didn't want to do anything to encourage him.

Or did she?

Against her better judgement, she marched back over to where he was sitting. "What are you trying to say?"

"I'm trying to say that *means* something."

You wish, she thought bitterly. The intensity of her anger surprised her and she made an effort to get her emotions under control. She softened her voice, an uncertain expression upon her face. "Johnny, we're on the side of a freeway. You . . ."

"Doesn't have to be here," he insisted. "How about dinner tonight? I know this great rib place."

She shook her head sadly. "It's not such a good idea."

"I thought maybe you might want an explanation," he said, "about what happened that day. The day I left."

His guilt and regret were painfully obvious. Roxanne

guessed that he had been beating himself up over his broken promise for way too long. She suddenly felt terrible about giving him such a hard time.

"Johnny," she said gently, "you were just seventeen. You witnessed a horrible tragedy and you ran. It made sense to me then, it makes sense to me now." After the initial shock of her abandonment, she'd had plenty of time to think things over and reach some sort of understanding about what had happened that day. "I have no hard feelings. None. The reason they call it the past is that, well, it's past. Over and done with." The more she talked about it, the more she almost believed it. "We're completely different people now than we were . . ."

Before she could finish, Johnny leaned forward and kissed her. His lips found hers and, for an endless moment, she was instantly transported back to a golden summer afternoon beneath a shady oak tree. Roxanne surrendered briefly to the kiss before she came to her senses and realized that this was neither the time nor the place. She reluctantly pulled away from him and shook her head. She turned back toward the van, striding a little less decisively this time. Her legs felt distinctly rubbery.

"It doesn't have to be ribs," he called out. "It could be Chinese, Italian . . . you name it."

She stopped, sighed, and looked back at him. Familiar hazel eyes entreated her. God, she could never resist those eyes. . . .

I'm going to regret this, she realized. "Okay, okay, fine.

There's a restaurant at my hotel—the Plaza. Eight o'clock."

His whole face lit up. "This is a sign, Roxanne!" he shouted exuberantly as she climbed back into the van. Stuart gave her a quizzical look, which she did her best to ignore. *It's just a dinner,* she rationalized, trying to convince herself that she hadn't just made a ghastly mistake. *Maybe a chance to achieve a little closure after all these years.* Her shrink would approve. Who knows? Perhaps she'd even get a good story out of this. Dinner with the famously reclusive Johnny Blaze. She knew reporters who'd sell their souls for an opportunity like that. . . .

The taste of his kiss lingered on her lips as the van pulled back into traffic. Passing motorists, recognizing Johnny in his snazzy white suit, honked their horns in greeting. Johnny waved back at them, looking almost embarrassingly happy.

Roxanne wondered what exactly she was getting into.

He wasn't the only one who took a big leap today.

8

A CLOCK ON THE WALL READ 7:15 P.M. JOHNNY'S DATE with Roxanne was still forty-five minutes away, but he had been ready for hours.

Sort of.

He'd showered, shaved, combed his hair, and (deciding to opt for casual attire) changed into his best black leather jacket, T-shirt, and jeans, yet he still had no idea what he was going to say to her when he finally got the chance. He paced nervously in front of an antique mirror mounted above the bathroom sink, practicing.

"Roxanne, that day, the day I left . . . well, the reason I did that—and I felt bad, horrible about it—but the reason was . . ." He hesitated, working up the nerve to say the actual words. ". . . well, I think I probably sold my soul to the Devil."

It was the first time he had ever said those words aloud, admitting what he had always suspected in his heart.

He couldn't believe how ridiculous it all sounded.

"No, that's no good," he realized, still pacing back and forth. "That's bad. This is going to be a disaster."

For a moment, he was half-tempted to call the whole thing off. If he had actually known Roxanne's cell phone number, he might have called to cancel. Maybe.

"No, no. Don't go there." He steeled himself to try again. "That's too negative. Gotta be positive. Power of positive thinking." God knows he'd read enough self-help books and spiritual guides on the subject. "I'm okay, you're okay. It's all going to be okay."

He stopped pacing and looked himself squarely in the mirror. His reflection showed him Johnny Blaze, stunt cyclist extraordinaire. Not a victim doomed to perpetual unhappiness because of a stupid mistake he made as a kid.

"You made that jump," he reminded himself. "Nobody else made that jump. You're the best rider and you deserve a second chance."

What was it he told Mack earlier today? "You can't live in fear."

Fishing a pack out of his pocket, he lit up a cigarillo to steady his nerves. His father's lung cancer hadn't stopped Johnny from picking up the habit. Then again, Barton Blaze had hardly died from cancer. Johnny rather suspected the same might apply to him. In his line of work, crash landings were more dangerous than nicotine.

Or maybe he just had a death wish.

To his surprise, the flame from his lighter *bent toward*

him. Johnny snapped the lighter shut and stared at it in bewilderment. He lifted a finger, but didn't detect any sort of draft that might explain the flame's odd behavior. The air was perfectly still.

Weird.

Before he could give the freakish phenomenon any more thought, a sudden heat rushed over his body.

His face flushed and he felt hot, feverish. Turning on the tap, he splashed cold water over his face, but the water did nothing to relieve the sudden increase in his temperature.

Johnny went to dry his hands on a towel, only to see the water instantly evaporate off his flesh, turning to steam right before his eyes. Heat radiated from his hand, causing the air around them to ripple like it did above hot asphalt on a particularly scorching day. *What the hell?* Johnny wondered. *I haven't been sick in years.*

A motorcycle engine revved outside the building. Johnny stiffened in shock. Even though he hadn't heard it in years, he'd recognize that distinctive rumble anywhere. He spun around and looked out the bathroom door at the cycle-crowded living quarters. His eyes zeroed in on one particular corner of the loft, already guessing what he would find there. Stacks of esoteric paperbacks and hardcovers had tumbled over onto a conspicuously empty stretch of floor space.

Grace was missing.

Zipping up his jacket, Johnny hurried down the steps

leading to the back exit. The familiar reverberation grew louder by the moment, drawing him out into the dimly lit alley behind the converted warehouse. Steel drums and wooden pallets were piled up against the outer wall. A dumpster was filled to overflowing with worn-out tires. Potholes defaced the pavement. He burst from the doorway, then froze in disbelief.

His father's motorcycle sat alone in the alley, looking as good as new for the first time in over a decade. The chopper's brilliant blue-and-yellow skin, and polished chrome, gleamed beneath the light from a street lamp outside the alley. The wheels were fully inflated once more. Every nick and scratch, every last bit of rust and corrosion, was gone. The Big Twin engines purred like a lion.

Even stranger, the bike was running by itself.

This is impossible, Johnny thought. His body still felt like it was burning up, and he wondered briefly whether the inexplicable fever was causing him to hallucinate. He reached out experimentally and found the bike solid to the touch. *This is no mirage*, he realized. *This is really happening.*

Grace's bright silver tank reflected his puzzled expression. Johnny gazed at his mirror-image, then jumped back in surprise when a *second* face appeared right behind him. A face he knew all too well.

Johnny spun around to face his past. "You . . ."

"Hello, Johnny," the stranger said.

Fifteen years had passed, but the man had not

changed a bit. Johnny recognized the same long black coat, swept-back blond hair, gold rings, and silver cane. He had just been a teenager when he last met the stranger at that lonely crossroads outside Sweetwater, but the other man did not appear to have aged a day. The crystal skull grinned at Johnny from atop the stranger's cane, looking pleased to see him.

"Get away from me," Johnny warned.

"Oh, it's a little late for that," the stranger replied.

Johnny had been dreading this moment for almost his entire adult life. Now that it was here, he could only back away from the stranger, putting Grace between them.

The two men circled the growling motorcycle in a kind of macabre dance. The stranger took his time, limping leisurely around the bike on his cane. He seemed to be enjoying the slow-motion chase.

"Nice bike," he commented.

Johnny was in no mood to talk shop. "Why are you here?" he asked fearfully.

"I've always been here, Johnny," the stranger answered. "All along. Phoenix. Denver. Houston. Seattle . . ."

A horrible thought occurred to Johnny. "Today. It was you. Keeping me alive." Maybe the success of his touchdown jump had nothing to do with his own talent as a rider. Maybe his entire career was a joke. "You're the reason I can—"

"Oh, no, Johnny." The stranger shook his head. "It's

all you. You're the best. And me? Well, I'm your biggest fan. The posters. The video games. The crowds chanting 'John-ny! John-ny! John-ny!'" He beamed at the younger man. "Makes me so proud. It's like watching an investment that keeps growing and growing . . . until the day you cash it in."

He regarded Johnny like a cat eying a tasty mouse. "That day is today, Johnny."

Grace's engines growled steadily louder. Heat waves radiated off its chassis and suspension.

"I want you to find the one known as Blackheart," the stranger said. "Bring him to me."

Blackheart? Who the hell is Blackheart?

"Do it yourself," he said defiantly.

"It doesn't work that way," the stranger answered. "You have the physical powers that I lack." Leaning upon his cane, he cast a rueful look at the heavens. "I am bound by the rules of the deal."

Johnny remembered the brown parchment scroll he had bled on so many years ago. "Another deal?" he said, the bitterness dripping from his voice.

The stranger smiled. "Always."

Well, I'm not playing by your rules anymore, Johnny thought. He swung his leg over Grace, preparing to ride off. After all, he had no intention of standing Roxanne up a second time. "I won't do it."

Before he could even twist the throttle, the bike's rear tire started spinning furiously. A cloud of blue smoke, better suited to a rocket launch than a motorcycle, vented from the Harley's exhaust pipes. Johnny instinctively grabbed onto the handlebars.

"You don't have any choice," the stranger said. He tapped his skull-headed cane against the pavement. Invisible bonds glued Johnny's hands to the handlebars. He tried to pull away, but it was like he was welded to the metal. Twisting the choke did nothing to quiet the Harley's revving engine.

VRRROOOOOMMM!

Grace rocketed out of the alley, taking Johnny with her. The jet-like thrust shoved him back in the saddle. He held onto the handlebars for dear life as the possessed chopper zoomed down the street.

. . . so fast that the asphalt was churned up in melted chunks.

. . . so fast that a fiery trail streaked the pavement behind him.

. . . so fast that his cheeks rippled from the g-forces he was pulling.

A helpless passenger on a breakneck ride across town, Johnny felt a scream tear itself from his lungs. The involuntary shriek was lost in the bike's deafening growl and the howl of the wind whipping past his exposed face. No crash helmet or visor protected his fragile human features. Bare hands gripped the handlebars so hard that his knuckles turned white.

For the first time ever, Johnny Blaze found himself riding so fast it scared him.

• • •

Roxanne arrived at the hotel restaurant ahead of Johnny. No real surprise there; she had been only a few floors away, not across town. She glanced at her wristwatch. 7:53. She expected he'd be here any minute.

Heads turned as the waiter guided her to a table for two. After way too much agonizing over what to wear, she had finally settled on a pleated skirt and a glitzy Vera Wang top. Not too formal, but not too casual either. A thin gold necklace and matching earrings accented her natural beauty. Chanel No. 5 added a touch of fragrance.

"Will someone else be joining you this evening?" the waiter asked.

"Yes," Roxanne said, smiling.

To her astonishment, she found she was actually looking forward to the dinner, and couldn't wait to see Johnny again.

Despite how it ended between them so many years ago, perhaps absence did make the heart grow fonder.

They had a lot to catch up on.

The speedometer clocked Grace's velocity at over two hundred miles per hour.

Skyscrapers warped past Johnny in a screaming blur of steel and glass. He squeezed hard on the brakes, but the out-of-control cycle didn't even slow down.

They blasted past a row of parked cars, whose side windows exploded in the Harley's wake, setting off a cacophony of shrieking car alarms all along several city blocks. A stream of fire trailed behind Grace like the tail of a comet. Heated blacktop bubbled and boiled.

A pothole sent a bone-shaking jolt through the berserk chopper. A license plate tore loose from the rear fender and went clattering down the middle of the lane before finally coming to rest in a gutter at the side of the road. Johnny didn't even notice it was gone.

Potted shrubs, planted along the sidewalks, burst into flame as Grace snicked into high gear. Parking meters drooped from the heat. Shattered shop windows sprayed glass onto the street. Parked vehicles, mercifully devoid of passengers, exploded into fireballs as their gas tanks ignited. Mangled metal rained down on the business district. Billowing clouds of black smoke rose from the wrecked vehicles.

The city streets looked like a war zone.

The bike and its unwilling passenger left downtown Fort Worth behind in a matter of minutes. Heading north, they burned rubber along Main Street, weaving recklessly through the evening traffic. Exerting all his strength, Johnny downshifted enough to keep his meteoric passage from setting the other cars ablaze. Startled drivers honked their horns and swore at the daredevil rider seemingly risking life and limb as the speeding Harley zipped in front and around the other vehicles, never slowing for a second. Even other motorcyclists gaped in amazement at Grace's wild ride. "Where's the fire, you freaking maniac?!" an angry biker shouted at the two-wheeled missile that had just left him in the dust.

A panicked Johnny wished he knew.

Ahead, a few miles up the road, a motorcycle cop hid behind a large wooden billboard. His left hand gripped a handlebar, while his right held up a raised speed gun. It had been a slow night so far; he had only ticketed two drivers for speeding and busted an embarrassed college kid for driving under the influence. He was hoping for a little more action before his shift was up.

A distant rumbling caught his attention. *That sounds promising,* he thought. He took aim with his speed gun and leaned forward on his bike. He gunned his engine just in case the perpetrator tried to make a run for it. His left heel raised the kickstand.

WHOOOOOOSH!

A bright blue Harley-Davidson rocketed past the road sign faster than the cop would have thought mechanically possible. "Holy crap!" he exclaimed. He glanced hurriedly at the read-out on the radar, which tracked the chopper's speed at 190 mph and climbing. The display burned out completely as the speed gun heated up in his grasp, then caught on fire. The cop yelped in pain and dropped the flaming device onto the ground. Only his thick leather gloves saved him from an instant third-degree burn. A blast of fiery exhaust knocked him onto the ground, as the entire billboard erupted into a raging inferno.

The shocked police officer scrambled away from the burning sign. He stared north in confusion, but the anonymous bike was already long gone. Only a long strip of burning asphalt, the blazing billboard, and the fried radar gun at his feet confirmed that the mystery cycle had ever existed in the first place.

The cop wondered how the hell he was ever going to explain this back at the station, even as, on the other side of the billboard, a helpful notice to DRIVE FRIENDLY—THE TEXAS WAY! went up in flames.

8:30. An empty glass of wine sat on the table in front of Roxanne. She checked her cell phone for messages. Nothing from Johnny. *Even if he couldn't get my number,* she thought impatiently, *he could have always called the hotel. He knows where I am.*

She stared at the entrance to the restaurant, hoping to see Johnny arrive at any minute. Each passing minute tugged at her heart. Her eyes watered as she admitted to herself just how much she had wanted—no, *needed*—to see Johnny tonight. Old wounds, that she had thought long healed, bled freshly into her soul. This was Crowley Hill all over again. . . .

The friendly waiter approached her table, looking sympathetic and slightly embarrassed. "May I get you anything else, miss?" he asked gently.

Screw this. She felt angry and humiliated and stupid. Roxanne had been a fool to ever give Johnny Blaze another chance to break her heart.

She stood up and threw a handful of bills onto the table. "No. *I'm done,*" she told the waiter emphatically before storming out of the restaurant.

9

THE OLD TRAIN STATION WAS LOCATED NORTH OF downtown, near the historic stockyards and meat-packing plants that had given Fort Worth its nickname of "Cowtown." The flavor of the Old West hung over the antique depot that had once serviced the Santa Fe line. An open courtyard, wide enough to accommodate delivery wagons and trucks, stretched between the two-story brick depot and the elevated wooden platform in front of the tracks. A diesel locomotive slumbered on the rails. The uneven floor of the courtyard was littered with dead leaves and muddy puddles. Train schedules and safety notices were posted on the exterior of the depot, along with a few old-time WANTED posters, just for color. Rusty chains dangled from the roof of an arched tunnel that ran through the center of the depot, connecting the courtyard with the parking lot beyond. A warm breeze rustled the fallen leaves. The air was hot and humid. A faraway train whistled several miles down the track.

Blackheart paid little attention to the station's

decor. Accompanied by the three elementals, he searched the deserted courtyard for clues to the location of his long-sought prize. No obvious marker presented itself.

But appearances could be deceiving. . . .

"Hey!" a braying voice interrupted his efforts. A portly mortal wearing a stationmaster's uniform came waddling toward them from the depot. "You can't come in here! This is private property!"

The man held up a kerosene lantern instead of a flashlight. A *traditionalist*, Blackheart concluded. *Just like Father.*

He disliked this human already.

The light from the lantern fell upon the sinister visages of the Hidden. The stationmaster blanched, his eyes bulging in fright behind a pair of bifocals. He backed away uneasily. The lantern dipped at the end of an unsteady arm.

It suddenly occurred to Blackheart that this timid mortal might possess some useful information. "There was a cemetery here," he prompted.

"Y-yeah," the human quavered. He acted like he was ready to bolt at the slightest provocation. "A long time ago."

Blackheart nodded. It seemed that his information, which he had taken pains to extract from the dog-eared pages of history, was correct. "What happened to the graves?"

"They were moved," the stationmaster said.

"Where?" Blackheart asked, his dark eyes narrowing.

"I dunno."

Blackheart frowned. That was not what he wanted to hear. He began to fear that he was wasting his time here. "Who would know?"

"St. Michael's Church. They were the ones in charge." The man's eyes shifted nervously from one demon to another, uncertain whom he should be most afraid of. He attempted to muster what little authority he had left. "You know, you really shouldn't be here."

Blackheart smiled as he stalked toward the stationmaster. "That's what they keep telling me."

He wondered what the chubby mortal would look like in blue.

Grace sped toward what looked like a closed train station. Johnny couldn't take any credit for riding here, nor for choosing their destination. The possessed chopper had driven like it had a mind of its own.

The bike screeched to a halt, throwing him from the saddle. He hit the pavement hard, then stumbled to his feet, grateful to be standing on his own two legs again. He would have kissed the ground if he hadn't been distracted by the raging furnace burning inside him.

The wind generated by his headlong ride across town had only slightly eased the feverish inferno that seemed to be consuming him. Now that Johnny was stationary once more, the volcanic heat quickly became unbearable. Rivulets of perspiration cascaded down his face. His face turned crimson. His blood felt like molten lava, coursing through his entire body. He stumbled across the empty parking lot, not knowing where he was or why he was there. As far as he knew, he was still in Texas, but it felt like he was already roasting in the fiery depths of hell. He threw back his head, crying out in agony.

"What's happening to me?!"

Tears of fire leaked from his eyes. The asphalt melted beneath his tread, so that he left a trail of smoldering boot prints sunk into the pavement. Johnny clutched his head as crackling coils of yellow flame snaked out of his blazing sockets. Smoke rose from his dark hair and eyebrows. Somewhere past the unbearable pain, his mind registered the smell of his own burning flesh.

Death would be a welcome relief.

Make it stop! he prayed. *For the love of God, please make it stop!*

His face ignited like burning parchment, the skin scorched from his skull as though from an explosion within.

No trace of Johnny Blaze's famous countenance remained; instead a bleached white skull, enveloped in a halo of dancing yellow flames, sat atop the leather-clad shoulders. Hellfire smoldered in the shadowy depths of his eye sockets.

The blazing figure should have been dead, yet it felt stronger than ever before. The scalding pain was just a fading memory.

The Ghost Rider had been reborn.

He raised a skeletal hand before him and clenched it into a fist. Power, and a newfound sense of purpose, surged through the marrow of his bones.

The waiting was over. He knew why he walked the Earth.

He had a duty to perform.

Blackheart drained the last paltry dregs of fear from the stationmaster's wizened blue corpse. Releasing his hold on the mummy's throat, he let the empty carcass drop onto the leaf-strewn courtyard. The man's kerosene lantern lay on the ground a few feet away, its sputtering flame slowly dying out.

I believe our business here is concluded. It was obvious that their prize was not to be found in this dismal setting, but at least the unfortunate mortal had pointed them in the right direction before outliving his usefulness. Blackheart intended to proceed to their next destination with no further delay. He turned to inform Abigor and the others—

Wait! Blackheart suddenly sensed another presence among them, one that he had been anticipating ever since confronting his father outside the biker bar.

Mephistopheles was finally making his move, albeit by proxy.

Blackheart glanced toward the archway leading to the courtyard. His ears detected a determined tread approaching. He glimpsed a flicker of hellfire at the far end of the tunnel.

"What is it?" Abigor asked.

Blackheart grinned in anticipation.

"The Rider."

Ghost Rider walked fearlessly through the archway into the courtyard in front of the railroad tracks.

Sarcastic applause greeted his arrival.

He spied Blackheart standing several paces ahead, seemingly quite alone. The husk of a murdered mortal lay upon the ground at the youth's feet. Papery blue skin indicated death by necroplasm.

"Looking for someone?" Blackheart asked, no longer clapping.

Ghost Rider knew his prey on sight. He pointed a bony finger at the devil's rebellious son. "*Violator*," he accused in an eerie, sepulchral voice that brooked no dissent. Blackheart had trespassed against the immutable laws of Hell. There would be a reckoning.

"You shouldn't be fighting me, Rider." Blackheart appealed to the bounty hunter's personal agenda. "We both want the same thing." He smiled slyly. "To be rid of Mephistopheles."

Johnny Blaze might have agreed, but the Ghost Rider could never be bargained with. He stepped decisively towards Blackheart. "*Back to Hell.*"

"I don't think so," Blackheart replied.

The wind whistled in Ghost Rider's nonexistent ear. A cyclonic gust of filthy air blasted against him, driving the bounty hunter back under the archway. The airborne grit would have scoured the flesh from his face, had any trace of skin still been present. Abigor's demonic face cackled within the swirling grit as the Spirit of Vengeance was blown back into the murky tunnel. A hanging chain wrapped around the naked vertebrae beneath his chin. The rusty iron noose threatened to break his neck.

Undaunted, Ghost Rider stayed upon his feet. He reached up and tugged the constricting chain away from his throat. With a savage motion, he yanked the chain free from the ceiling and turned his attention back to Blackheart.

Chain in hand, he marched toward the errant demonspawn. His heavy black boot splashed down into a greasy puddle—and stuck there. His glowing sockets looked down at the turbid waters and saw two liquid hands holding onto his foot. Wallow's vulpine features rippled across the surface of the puddle. Ghost Rider tried to pull his leg free, but the elemental's soggy grip held him fast.

He raised the chain, intending to lash out at his watery captor, only to be distracted by the sudden roar of a powerful engine. The burning skull pivoted on its neckbone in time to see a massive tractor-trailer barreling across the courtyard toward the trapped specter. Black smoke billowed from the eighteen-wheeler's exhaust stack. The grille of the truck slammed into Ghost Rider, propelling him across the train tracks into the parked locomotive. The sound of metal smashing violently rang out across the station. The front of the semi folded inward like an accordion. Hot steam billowed from the crumpled hood.

The cabin door swung open and Gressil stepped out onto the tracks. The earth elemental was unharmed by the crash. Thick black smoke obscured the site of the collision, where the Rider had presumably been flattened between the truck and the train. A leering grin exposed a mouthful of dirty brown teeth.

"He weren't so tough," the demon said.

Turning his back on the train, he started to walk back toward the station. He had only taken a few steps, however, before a skeletal hand clamped down on his shoulder. Gressil spun around in shock to see Ghost Rider standing right behind him in all his preternatural fearsomeness. The vengeful entity drew back his fist and threw a haymaker punch that knocked off a chunk of the elemental's face and sent Gressil flying through the air to crash to the ground over twenty feet away. The demon landed face-first amidst the scattered leaves and litter. He scrambled to his feet, still reeling from the unexpected and awesome impact of the Rider's blow.

"*Please!*" he begged. Shattered teeth fell like gravel onto the floor of the courtyard. His yellow eyes were filled with fear. "*Have mercy!*"

Ghost Rider raised his chain. Hellfire ignited along the length of it, causing the heavy metal links to take on a red-hot glow.

"No mercy for me," he proclaimed. *"No mercy for you!"*

He cracked the blazing chain like a bullwhip. The burning links snapped out and lassoed the squirming demon. Gressil howled in agony as he burst into flame. Eldritch fire heated the elemental's body, hardening it into solid obsidian. Ghost Rider yanked back the chain and Gressil shattered into a thousand pieces. The brittle stone cracked loudly, sounding like an explosion in a china shop. Only a cascade of broken shards and a whiff of burnt charcoal testified that Gressil had ever walked the earth at all.

No more Hiding for him, Ghost Rider thought.

He snapped the chain back to him. It wrapped itself across his torso like a bandoleer as its incendiary radiance dimmed. Looking away from the elemental's cremated remains, Ghost Rider scanned the grounds of the station for his other quarries. But Blackheart and the two surviving elementals were gone.

No matter, he resolved. He would pursue the fugitive demons across the face of the earth if needs be.

And not on foot.

Ghost Rider waved his fist in the air, beckoning silently to his ride. The roar of a motorcycle responded to his summons as, riderless, Grace came racing through the archway to his side.

The venerable Harley-Davidson was an impressive machine, but not fully sufficient to his purposes. Yet that could be easily remedied.

He laid a bony hand upon the chopper's rear exhaust pipe. Hellfire spread from his fingers across the length of the bike, transforming it beneath his touch. Solid metal twisted into new and more intimidating configurations. The handlebars took on the semblance of writhing serpents. The front fairing assumed the aspect of a large demonic skull. Blazing sockets flared instead of a headlight. The chrome forks connecting the frame to the front tires turned into taut steel chains. Grace's blue-and-yellow paint job was replaced by a glossy black luster. The entire chassis suddenly resembled the sculpted vertebrae of some unearthly beast. The tires ignited into flame, changing into rings of literally burning rubber. Bright orange flames crackled above the spinning wheels.

Within seconds, the customized Harley had become something else, a ride unique upon the Earth and elsewhere: the Hellcycle.

Ghost Rider withdrew his hand and mounted the bike. Its supercharged engine snarled like a wild animal as he opened up the throttle and raced away from the lifeless train station. Unlike Johnny Blaze's involuntary trip here, this time the satanic cycle was firmly under its rider's control. The Hellcycle sped off into the night, leaving behind a melted maelstrom of licking flames and burning asphalt.

The quarry could run, but it couldn't hide.

The Ghost Rider was hot on its trail.

10

EDDIE DELGADO LURKED IN AN ALLEY OFF SUNDANCE Square. He needed cash—fast—and wasn't too picky about how he got it. He peered around the corner, looking for a likely prospect.

A grin came across his stubble-covered face as he spotted a teenage Goth chick heading down the sidewalk toward him, no doubt on her way home from a long night of clubbing. Oblivious to her surroundings, she swayed to the rhythm of whatever morbid ditty was playing over her iPod. A tight black T-shirt warned: I LEAVE BITE MARKS. Her frizzy hair was dyed pitch-black. Racoon makeup shadowed her eyes. Her ivory complexion looked like it hadn't seen the sun in ages. A silver ankh dangled on a chain around her neck. Studded wristbands adorned her pudgy arms. Apparently alone, she had the brick-paved sidewalk to herself.

Eddie's bloodshot eyes zoomed in on the shining Egyptian amulet, as well as the lacy black handbag slung over her shoulder. He wondered how much money she was carrying, and what he might be able to get for her jewelry. Darting back behind the corner, he listened to her footsteps drawing nearer. His fingers tightened on the grip of a rusty Bowie knife. He waited until she came into view, then pounced on her from behind. She yelped in surprise and he clamped his hand over her mouth and dragged her roughly into the unlit alley.

Eddie slammed her up against a graffiti-covered stone wall. His hefty body pressed against her, pinning her to the wall. He held the knife to her throat, while his free hand yanked the bag from her shoulder. She squirmed helplessly, unable to get away. Some sort of exotic perfume tickled his nostrils.

"Shut up and be still!" he hissed into her ear. "Or I'll kill you!"

Her eyes bulged in terror. She trembled uncontrollably.

The girl's obvious distress and vulnerability turned Eddie on. He sniffed her hair, inhaling another deep breath of her fragrance, as he considered the possibilities of this situation. He had only intended to rob this chick, but . . . now that he had her alone in the alley, he found he wanted more than just the contents of her purse. She wasn't bad-looking, once you got past all the spooky Goth crap. Who knew? Maybe he'd even let her live afterward. . . .

The roar of an approaching motorcycle broke into his lustful fantasies. He glanced back over his shoulder, just to make sure they weren't going to be interrupted, and started to haul the teenager deeper into the alley. He froze in his tracks, however, as *a skull-headed biker rode past the alley on a flaming chopper.*

"What the f—?"

He exchanged a startled look with his victim, who seemed similarly stunned by the bizarre apparition. *Did we really just see that?*

Maybe he should just grab the girl's money and run?

But it was already too late. The blazing cycle, along with its spectral rider, backed up in front of the alley. The skull-headed biker got off the chopper and stood ominously at the mouth of the filthy passageway. Lambent flames danced around his fleshless cranium like a demonic halo. His burning sockets stared at Eddie and his intended victim.

"Oh, crap," the hoodlum muttered. Sensing he had real trouble on his hands, he released the girl, who quickly dashed away from him. She hesitated momentarily between Eddie and the ghostly motorcyclist, apparently uncertain who represented the greater threat, then decided to take her chances with the devil she didn't know. Her awestruck eyes got a good look at the eerie biker as she sprinted past him as quickly as she could manage on her tottering heels. Frantic footsteps receded into the distance, leaving Eddie alone with the rider. The nightmarish entity paid no heed to the girl's departure. His fearsome gaze remained fixed on the trembling mugger.

"W-who the hell are you, man?" Eddie demanded. The knife trembled in his grip. "What's your problem?"

"*I'm Ghost Rider,*" the specter replied. His stentorian voice emerged from the open jaws of the burning skull.

This was too much for Eddie. He turned and ran, desperate to be anywhere but here. Startled rats scurried beneath an overstuffed garbage Dumpster to get out of his way. Broken glass crunched beneath his feet. The bottom rung of a rusty metal fire escape beckoned to him, and he jumped onto a trash can to try to reach the hanging ladder. His fingers closed around the painted steel bar and he felt a surge of hope as he started to pull himself upward onto the fire escape.

He was going to get away!

Eddie's blood suddenly turned to ice as the Ghost Rider's skeletal hand grabbed onto the back of his belt. With unbelievable strength, he pulled Eddie back down onto the floor of the alley. He spun the mugger around so that Eddie had no choice but to stare right into the skull's blazing eyes.

In a panic, Eddie stabbed his knife into the monster's shoulder. The blade sliced through Ghost Rider's leather jacket, but was quickly consumed by the hellish flames blazing underneath the leather. Eddie yelped in pain as the knife turned red-hot. Molten metal dripped onto the pavement. He hastily dropped the knife, leaving him unarmed and defenseless before the wrath of the ghastly avenger.

It was the single most terrifying moment of Eddie Delgado's pathetic life.

Ghost Rider pronounced judgment on his wretched soul:

"*GUILTY!*"

The burning skull was only inches away from Eddie's own face. He tried to tear his eyes away, but the cavernous black sockets seemed to suck him in. At first, he saw only the plutonic flames burning where the skull's eyes should have been, but, within a heartbeat, *faces* began to appear within the roiling fires.

The faces of all the men, women, and children he had ever abused over the course of his short, brutal existence.

He recognized the wrinkled Russian widow he had mugged on her way home from church, the four-eyed geek he had beaten the crap out of in junior high, the asshole he'd stabbed in that bar fight, the ex-girlfriend he used to slap around, the witness he'd crippled for testifying against him, the "dates" he had forced himself upon, the yuppie tourists whose bodies would never be found, the homeless guy he set on fire, the fags whom he and his buddies had put in the hospital that one time, and so many others, more than he could even remember, names and faces that he thought he had long forgotten. The endless string of victims blurred into a gory montage of pain and suffering. Their pitiful cries and whimpers echoed inside his own skull, adding to the downward spiral of his already-slipping sanity.

"*Your soul is stained by the blood of the innocent,*" Ghost Rider declared. "*Feel their pain. . . .*"

The tortured faces merged into a single contorted visage that Eddie almost didn't recognize as his own. He opened his mouth to scream, but all that escaped his lungs was a thin, plaintive whistle, like the air being let out of leaky tire. His limbs refused to move. He felt paralyzed from the neck down.

"*. . . A hundred fold.*"

All at once, Eddie felt every act of violence, every evil he had ever committed, revisited upon him . . . with interest. A phantom knife twisted in his gut, invisible blows rained down on him, illusory flames seared his skin. Every inch of his body cried out in torment. A lifetime's worth of fear and guilt left his conscience raw and bleeding.

He dropped onto the trash-strewn floor of the alley. Shuddering from head to toe, he curled up into a fetal position. A low moan keened from his lips.

Eddie Delgado's glassy eyes stared inward into what remained of his soul, reliving his copious sins forevermore.

Ghost Rider left him lying there.

A wrought-iron fence surrounded the old cemetery, which was several miles west of the urban metroplex. Weathered tombstones and mausoleums rose from the parched soil. Tall grass and weeds clotted the overgrown graveyard. Dawn was rising as Ghost Rider motored up to the open gate, drawn by a powerful compulsion he didn't fully understand. The Hellcycle's engine began to sputter as the sun's rays fell upon the infernal chopper.

Night, and night alone, was the Rider's rightful domain.

The Hellcycle chugged to a halt just inside the cemetery. Ghost Rider stumbled off the bike and tottered woozily upon his feet. An overpowering weakness washed over him in conjunction with the rising sun. He reached out for a nearby headstone, hoping to steady himself, but his strength evaporated with the dawn. He toppled forward onto the ground, hitting the earth with a clatter of bones. Unwilling to relinquish his hold on existence, he crawled across the graveyard, dragging himself towards the shade of a large marble monument. His flaming aura began to sputter weakly.

The merciless sunlight brought on a bizarre transformation. Fresh skin spread over the naked skull. Thick black hair sprouted from his bony dome. The burning embers within his eye sockets congealed into confused hazel orbs. It was like watching a burning cadaver decompose in reverse. The eldritch flames died out.

Johnny Blaze lifted his shaky head from the ground. Bleary-eyed, he looked about in confusion. He tried to lift himself from the dirt, but exhaustion overcame him. His trembling limbs would not support him and he collapsed onto the earth. His eyelids drooped shut.

The sound of a shovel striking the ground, only a

few inches away from his head, briefly roused him. Johnny looked up to see a tall, masculine figure looming over him, leaning against the handle of the shovel. Silhouetted against the rising sun, the man's feature's were obscured by the glare, but Johnny got an impression of a grizzled cowboy who looked like he had just stepped out of an old Louis L'Amour novel. A battered brown Stetson sat atop the man's brow. He spat a mouthful of tobacco juice on ground.

"Mornin', bonehead."

His gruff voice sounded distinctly unimpressed.

Who?

Johnny passed out at the man's feet.

11

THE FIRST THING JOHNNY BLAZE SAW UPON WAKING was an angel hovering over him. He blinked at the surreal image, then realized that he was staring up at a stained-glass portrait of St. Michael, complete with heavenly wings and a flaming sword. Looking around, he discovered that he was lying on a cot inside a dimly lit shack. An open door looked out upon a dilapidated old graveyard that he vaguely remembered from the night before.

His head was pounding with the mother of all hangovers and his mouth felt as dry as the Mojave. Sitting up, he found a half dozen glasses of water lined up on a bedside table. He gratefully chugged the water down. It helped . . . a little.

Confused and disoriented, he rolled off the cot and onto his feet. He started to stand up, only to be overcome by a sudden wave of dizziness. The shack seemed to spin around him and he hurriedly dropped back down onto the cot. He sat with his head between his knees, waiting for the spinning sensation to stop.

Wincing in pain, he realized that he hurt like hell, like he'd been hit by a truck.

Maybe he had.

The dizziness passed and he stood up again. This time he managed to stay upright, although his head still felt like it was burning up. Looking for answers, he staggered out of the shack.

Crumbling marble monuments populated the cemetery grounds. Old-fashioned tombstones, their inscriptions half worn away by the passage of time, jutted from the earth at odd angles, like teeth badly in need of orthodontia. The large brick shack, with its stained-glass windows and shingled roof, squatted amidst the crypts and headstones. A crude timber cross was plastered to one side of the shack. A heavy wooden door guarded its interior. High grass threatened to overrun the cemetery, which had definitely seen better days. The whole place had a distinctly Boot Hill vibe.

Dirt and gravel clattered on the ground nearby. Johnny looked over to see an older man digging a grave a few yards away. Dusty brown work clothes covered the man's tall, rangy frame. A cowboy hat protected his grizzled face from the hot afternoon sun. A bandana was tied around his neck. A small silver cross dangled on a chain from his open vest. He scooped up another load of dirt with his shovel and tossed it to one side. Johnny dimly remembered seeing this same man earlier, right before he lost consciousness.

A thousand questions rushed through Johnny's

brain. *Where am I? What am I doing here?* Fevered memories of hellfire and demons and unearthly vengeance flashed across his mind. He looked anxiously at his hands, half expecting to see nothing but naked bones emerging from his sleeves. His fingers explored the contours of his face, relieved to feel the warm skin covering his skull. *That was just a nightmare, right? Nothing that really happened.*

Did it?

The sunlight hurt his eyes.

"Y'all right?" the old-timer asked, observing his discomfort. He turned away from the grave, still clutching his shovel with both hands.

Johnny shrugged. "I'm good." Perspiration dotted his brow. "Feels like my skull's on fire. But I'm good."

The other man chuckled to himself.

"Did I say something funny?" Johnny asked irritably.

"Not funny, ironic." Silver hair hung beneath the brim of the man's hat, matching his bushy mustache and beard. Gravedust accumulated in the deep creases of his face. The man was sixty if he was a day, yet looked tougher than most men half his age. "We're big on irony here."

He ambled toward Johnny, still toting his dirt-stained shovel.

"Folks call me Caretaker."

Suddenly remembering something, Johnny looked anxiously around the cemetery. Where had his ride gone?

"I put your bike behind the shack," Caretaker said, as if reading Johnny's mind. He nodded at the one-story brick structure.

My bike, Johnny thought. Spinning wheels of fire raced across his memory. He stared at the shack, wishing he could see straight through its sturdy walls to the other side. *Does Grace look normal . . . or like something else?*

"It does," Caretaker said.

Johnny gave the man a startled look. "What?"

"You're wonderin' if it looks normal," Caretaker confirmed with unnerving accuracy. "It does." He swung the shovel off his shoulder and stuck it into the ground in front of him. "And to answer your other questions . . . last night *did* happen, it wasn't a dream, and it will happen again."

How does he know all this? Johnny wondered. He stared at Caretaker, not understanding what was happening. "Who are you?"

The older man shrugged. "The question is: who are *you?*"

Who or what. There was nothing human about some of the febrile memories of the night before. He started walking toward the shack, wanting to check on Grace for himself. He wondered how far he was from his loft back in Fort Worth. Home was sounding better and better. Home and . . .

Roxanne! He suddenly realized that he had stood her up once again, just like he had back at Crowley Hill so many years ago. He was supposed to meet her at the restaurant last night, before . . . everything happened. *She's never going to speak to me again, let alone give us another chance.* He pondered the horror show his life had just become.

Maybe it's just as well.

Caretaker gave Johnny a stern look. He wasn't done with him yet.

"You're the Rider, kid. Get used to it. It's easier that way. If you don't . . ." He gestured toward the open grave. ". . . got a cozy spot picked out for you."

Johnny decided he'd heard enough. All he wanted was to get out of here and forget that any of this had ever happened. He circled around the shack to where Grace was standing amidst the underbrush. A heavy chain was wrapped around the sissy bar at the rear of the saddle.

Caretaker followed him around the shack. He seemed intent on making Johnny fully aware of the cold, cruel realities of his new existence. Who knew what his motive was.

"They've seen you now. They know what to expect. You'll need my help if you expect to last the night."

Johnny was dubious. "Last time I let a stranger help me, it didn't pan out so good."

He climbed onto Grace and fired up the engine.

"This ain't something you can run from, kid." Caretaker rammed his shovel into the dirt. "This day's been comin' ever since you made a *deal* by putting a drop of your blood on that paper."

Despite himself, Johnny instantly recalled that long-ago evening in the ice-cold maintenance tent. His fingertip tingled where the stranger's parchment had sliced through his flesh the night before Barton Blaze died. He started to ride away, then looked back over his shoulder. Maybe Caretaker knew what he was talking about? He sure seemed to know enough about how this nightmare got started.

Johnny hit the brakes and killed the motor.

"Congratulations," Caretaker said laconically. "Your chances just went from none to slim."

Yellow crime-scene tape cordoned off the train station, keeping out the competing news teams mobbing around the site. Roxanne stood in front of the tape, with the antiquated depot positioned behind her, as she held up her microphone and spoke directly into the camera.

". . . sources close to the investigation confirm that there may be links between what happened here in the downtown historic district and the 'Fallen Angels' massacre in the desert outside the city."

"And we're out," Stuart announced. The cameraman looked away from the viewfinder and gave her the "okay" sign.

Roxanne lowered her mike and looked around. There had to be more to this story, she guessed, than the police were letting on. Why would a rival biker gang want to murder the night manager at an obsolete old train depot? She was grateful for the potential scoop; it gave her something to concentrate on besides Johnny's no-show last night.

An older man with gray hair and a severe expression was leaving the site. She recognized Captain Gerard Dolan of the Fort Worth Police Department, whom she had interviewed once before. Signaling Stuart to follow her, she hustled toward him, mike in hand. The cameraman hurried after her, already starting filming.

"Captain Dolan?" She caught up with the veteran cop just as he stepped past the yellow tape. A rumpled suit and tie distinguished Dolan from the uniformed officers under his command. She shoved her mike toward him. "Roxanne Simpson—"

"No comment," he said brusquely. Judging from his expression, he wasn't having a good day.

Roxanne wasn't taking no for an answer. "Is it true they've found a connection between the Biker Bar Massacre and last night's victim found here in the train yards?"

"No comment." Dolan glowered at the camera in his face.

Roxanne waved Stuart away. Getting the message, he switched the camera off. "Look, off the record, okay?"

"Off the record?" Dolan looked her in the eye. "Piss off."

He turned and stalked toward a waiting patrol car.

Asshole, Roxanne thought. "I have friends in the department. . . ."

"I'm not one of them," Dolan snapped.

A younger detective scurried over to the captain, clutching a manila folder. Roxanne was almost positive his name was Edwards. Clean-cut and neatly groomed, he looked less irascible than his boss. She had heard about him from some of the local stringers. Energetic and ambitious, was the word on the street.

"Forensics on the bikers and stationmaster came back with the exact same cause of death," he reported eagerly. He handed the folder to his boss, who paused to leaf through the lab reports. Dolan squinted at the bottom line.

" 'Sulfur poisoning'?" he read aloud. His brow furrowed in confusion. "I didn't think sulfur was toxic."

"It is in massive doses," Edwards explained. "And these stiffs are *swimming* in it. Could be evidence of a chemical attack?"

"Or a religious nut," Roxanne interjected.

The two cops turned around to find the reporter standing right behind him. Dolan obviously thought he had already left her behind. *Sometimes it pays to have a light step*, she thought, *especially when you need to listen in on something you weren't meant to hear.*

Edwards's eyes widened at the sight of the attractive newswoman. "Hey, I know you!" he blurted. "I've seen you on—"

Dolan silenced the young detective with a glare. He reluctantly turned to deal with Roxanne. "There's nothing here to suggest any kind of religious M.O."

Roxanne disagreed. "The sulfur," she pointed out. "Or, as it was known back in the day, *brimstone.*"

She savored the policemen's flummoxed expressions. It amused her that neither man had made the satanic connection yet.

How's that for investigative reporting?

Sunlight filtered through the stained-glass windows of Caretaker's shack. Lighted candles dispelled whatever shadows remained, revealing spartan quarters that boasted little in the way of modern appliances or conveniences. The meager furnishings included a cot, an old-fashioned roll-top desk, and a wood-burning stove that probably saw little use during the summer. An unfinished game of solitaire rested atop a plain wooden table. A calendar, showcasing the Western art of Frederic Remington, was pinned to one wall. There was no TV, no computer, no telephone, no air-conditioning. A pot of water simmered upon hot plate. A horseshoe was nailed over the door. The whole place had an austere, almost monastic feel to it.

Johnny guessed that Caretaker didn't get out much.

The biker's leather jacket was draped over the back of the antique wooden chair he was sitting on. His left sleeve was rolled up as far as it would go. A bloody gash scarred his shoulder. He vaguely recalled a crazed hoodlum stabbing him with a knife. The injury hadn't affected Ghost Rider at all, but this morning Johnny was definitely feeling it. The ugly wound throbbed painfully.

"The Rider is the Devil's bounty hunter," Caretaker explained as he tended to Johnny's shoulder. Hydrogen peroxide stung like fire as he cleaned out the wound. "Sent to hunt down anything that escapes from Hell." He held up a stainless steel needle. "Sterilize this for me."

Johnny eyed the needle. He remembered the hellfire that he had wielded as Ghost Rider, how it had flowed from his body into his chain and motorcycle, infusing them with demonic power. He tentatively reached out and pressed his finger against the needle.

Nothing happened.

Caretaker chuckled and nodded toward the hot plate. "Try the boiling water."

Feeling slightly embarrassed, Johnny got up and dipped the tip of the needle into the water bubbling in the dented tin pot. He handed the needle back to Caretaker. *How am I supposed to know what the rules are?* he thought defensively. *None of this makes any sense!*

Except that it did.

Caretaker spelled it out for him. "During the day, you'll be normal. But at night, in the presence of evil, the Rider takes over." He attached a slender thread to the needle and started to stitch up the gash. Johnny flinched, but didn't pull away. He bit down on his lower lip as the older man continued his explanation.

"The last time was one hundred and fifty years ago, in a little Mexican village called San Venganza. Used to be a nice town, nice people, until a stranger came along promising wealth and prosperity, one deal at a time. One fella pricks his finger and signs, gets rich. Others see that, they sign, too. Everyone signs." He sighed in recollection. "But pretty soon nobody loves nuthin' but what's in their pocket, or their neighbor's pocket, or their neighbor's bed. . . ."

He pulled the thread taut and kept on stitching. Johnny ignored the pain, caught up in the old-timer's narrative. He knew just what kind of deals Caretaker was talking about, and he had a pretty good idea he knew who the stranger was, too. The name popped into his brain from last night's encounter at the train station—Blackheart had called the Devil "Mephistopheles."

It was as good a name as any.

"Where evil lives," Caretaker went on, "nothing grows. No crops, no trees, no children. The town's dying. The well runs dry. They curse the stranger with their dying breaths, their cursed souls trapped forever in that godforsaken place."

Johnny could believe it. *Sounds like the people of San Venganza got screwed over in the deal the same way I did.* Barton Blaze's untimely death still haunted his dreams.

"What does this have to do with Blackheart?" he asked.

"Blackheart?" Caretaker froze in mid-stitch, taken aback by the name. "He sent you after Blackheart?"

Johnny nodded. "Along with some others."

"The Hidden," Caretaker guessed, his expression grim. "Fallen angels cast out of Heaven by St. Michael himself." He glanced up at the stained-glass window. He finished stitching up the wound and bit off the end of the thread; obviously he'd done this before. "You should stay here. They can't set foot on hallowed ground."

Johnny wondered if that was why Caretaker lived here. What was his involvement in this whole business anyway? *What's his stake in all this?*

Who the hell is this guy anyway? How does he know all this?

"Great," Johnny said sarcastically. "I feel so much better now that I know I'm the Devil's bounty hunter." He got up and put his jacket back on.

Caretaker frowned. "Where are you going?"

"There's someone I got to see," Johnny said. Even if Roxanne never wanted to have anything to do with him again, he couldn't just disappear from her life without explanation again. He had made that mistake back in 1989, and had spent the last fifteen years regretting it. *I have to talk to her one more time, if only to say good-bye.*

"That's a bad idea," Caretaker said.

Johnny shrugged. "Wouldn't be my first."

He headed for the door. Caretaker followed him out into the graveyard, where Grace stood waiting. Johnny worried that the gritty-looking old-timer might try to physically stop him from leaving, but Caretaker seemed to sense that Johnny's mind was made up. Johnny was grateful that the old gravedigger respected his decision.

"Hey," Caretaker said just as Johnny was about to climb onto the bike. He turned around to see what the other man wanted. "Why'd you do it? Why'd you make the deal?"

Johnny didn't want to get into it. "I was just a kid."

"What'd you get in return?" Caretaker asked.

That was an easy one.

"Heartache," Johnny replied.

12

As Johnny rode home through downtown Fort Worth, there was no ignoring the damage left behind by his hellish ride the night before. Scorch marks scarred the congealed asphalt. Burning wheels had left deep furrows down the middle of lanes. Parked cars and trucks had been turned into burned-out hulks, many lying upside-down or in pieces. A twisted fender protruded from the punctured wall of a small Savings and Loan building. Broken windows had been boarded-over. Melted parking meters drooped toward the sidewalk. A billboard had been reduced to a couple of charred wooden posts. Potted shrubs were burned to a crisp. A postman scraped heaps of ashes out of a metal mailbox. Insurance investigators were either going to shake their heads in bewilderment or hit the bars early.

All because of me, Johnny thought. *Or rather, Ghost Rider.*

A familiar blue news van was parked at the curb just past Sundance Square. Slowing down, Johnny was surprised to see Roxanne standing in front of an alley, interviewing a teenage Goth chick. He came to a stop and parked his bike right behind the van. Intent on getting their story, neither Roxanne nor her cameraman noticed as he approached them on foot. Although anxious to speak with her, Johnny kept a respectful distance away from the alley, not wanting to interrupt Roxanne at work. He quietly listened in on the interview.

"Can you describe the Good Samaritan to us?" Roxanne asked the teenager. Johnny thought the girl looked vaguely familiar. *Do I know her?*

She nodded. "I'll never forget him, that's for sure. He was tall, broad shoulders, thin . . . super thin, like bony . . . and he had this really rad chopper. It was all flames and stuff." She searched her memory for more details. "Oh, and his face was a skull and it was on fire."

Johnny suddenly remembered where he knew the girl from. *Last night, in this very alley.* He instinctively backed away, as if afraid of being recognized. *She's describing . . . me.*

"On fire?" Roxanne was momentarily thrown off by the girl's response.

"Yeah, like . . ." She held her hands up around her head, pantomiming an invisible halo. "Like this much fire." She shrugged at Roxanne's bewildered expression. "I know it sounds weird, but it looked okay on him. I mean, it's an edgy look, sure, but he pulled it off."

Good to know, Johnny thought wryly.

Roxanne turned toward the camera. "Not sure what to add to that," she admitted, trying to present a light tone. "I'm Roxanne Simpson, on the scene of an aborted mugging. The alleged perpetrator, one Eddie Delgado, is currently undergoing psychiatric evaluation after being found in a near-comatose state earlier this morning."

Stuart lowered the camera and started loading his gear back into the van. Roxanne thanked the girl for her cooperation . . . then noticed Johnny at last. Her face froze into an icy mask.

"Roxanne," he said, stepping toward her. "Last night I was on my way, I swear, but—"

She held up her hand. "Stop! No apologies." Behind her unforgiving expression, fifteen years of pent-up anger smoldered in her dark eyes and voice. "You did me a favor. Because it forced me to think about then . . . and now. When you left me standing at that tree, sure, it hurt like hell. But I got over it, went to college, got a great job, started a promising career." She looked him over like he was something she had found stuck to the bottom of her shoe. "But you, Johnny, you're the same. Better pay, more fans . . . but you're still just a carny."

The accusation hit Johnny hard, worse than any mugger's knife or speeding semi. No supernatural powers shielded him from the scorn in her voice. He probably deserved every word.

"My dad was right, Johnny. You were a phase."

Johnny felt his last golden memories going up in flames. *So much for second chances*, he mournfully thought. Mephistopheles had pretty much driven a stake through that pipe dream. How could he ever ask Roxanne to be with him now that he was the Devil's own bounty hunter?

"He *was* right," Johnny agreed. "We can't be together."

Roxanne looked like she was surprised, and maybe even a little disappointed, at how quickly Johnny had given up on her. Shaking her head, she turned away and slowly marched back toward the van.

She got into the van and drove away.

Johnny could only stand there and let her go.

Several blocks away, a forensic examiner inspected the charred pavement on the street leading to the train station. He spotted a crumpled piece of metal lying in a gutter at the side of the road. The criminalist tugged a blackened steel plate free from the congealed asphalt.

"Got something!" he yelled to his supervisor.

He wiped the soot from the evidence with his sleeve, confirming its identity.

It was a license plate, all right.

The sun was slowly sinking on the horizon, causing ominous black shadows to stretch out upon the grounds of the old cemetery. The man who called himself Caretaker took note of the approaching twilight as he carefully wiped the bird droppings off a weathered granite tombstone that rested in the shade of a gnarled hickory tree. The tree's branches had been stripped clean by the wind, but unlike many of the other graves around them, this particular mound had been kept free of dust, weeds, and fallen leaves. The inscription upon the tombstone read:

CARTER SLADE
1806–1866
Into Paradise May Angels Lead You

Caretaker read the inscription, even though he knew it by heart, then glanced back over his shoulder at a statue of St. Michael standing guard over the lonely cemetery. Caretaker rose, tucking his cleaning rag back into his pocket. He spat a wad of tobacco juice onto the dirt, then surveyed the grounds, just like he did every evening.

Everything seemed in order.

He tipped his Stetson at St. Michael as he headed over to his shack. His flinty eyes watched the sun set in the west. Deep red and purple bands suffused the sky above the horizon. The shadows thrown by the scattered tombstones grew longer by the second. It was almost time for Ghost Rider to ride again.

He wondered what Johnny Blaze was up to.

• • •

Johnny stared into the mirror at his loft.

He ran his fingers through his hair, finding it firmly rooted to his scalp. Skin still covered his skull. Hazel eyes gazed back at him, as opposed to burning black sockets. He let out a sigh of relief.

So far, so good.

Leaving the bathroom, he went back to his library. Grace rested on the cement floor of the loft, surrounded by disorganized piles of occult texts, many of them lying open to one page or another. Johnny had been poring through the tomes all afternoon, looking for more information on Mephistopheles, Blackheart, and their demonic cronies. He extracted all the books on the Devil and Satanism from the general New Age clutter. Squatting down on the floor, Johnny flipped through the pages in a hurry, scanning the titles and chapter headings in search of anything that might help him get through the coming night. *The Grand Grimoire. The Lesser Key of Solomon. Pseudomonarchia Daemonum.* Had Caretaker read any of these same books? The cagy old-timer sure seemed to know his stuff where deals with the Devil were concerned.

"Unhappy spirits that fell with Lucifer,

"Conspired against our God with Lucifer,

"And are forever damned with Lucifer."

Johnny skimmed the relevant passage in Marlowe's *Doctor Faustus.* He ripped out the page and added it to a growing stack of papers that also included choice extracts from Dante's *Inferno, The Book of Revelation,*

Paradise Lost, Memoirs of the Golden Dawn, and the *Malleus Malificarum*. He didn't waste time looking for a way out of his deal with Mephistopheles; if there was loophole to be found in these texts, he would have found it years ago.

Was there a single book on demonology I didn't read?

Finally, in a rose-colored leather bound volume titled *The Rise of the Midnight Son*, he stumbled onto an unsettling illustration. A centuries-old woodcut showed a youthful figure that somewhat resembled Blackheart, holding up his arms as a teeming swarm of evil souls were drawn into his body. Gothic type warned that "the Beast heralds the End of Days."

Johnny didn't like the sound of that.

He lingered over the foreboding illustration, taking in every detail. Could this have anything to do with the conflict between Blackheart and Mephistopheles? And where exactly did the Ghost Rider fit in?

A bell from the elevator startled him. Someone was coming up to the loft. Johnny flagged the page with the woodcut on it, then climbed to his feet. His legs ached from sitting in the same position too long. His shoulder itched where Caretaker had stitched up his wound. He walked over to face the elevator door.

Who could this be? he wondered. *Mack?*

Somehow he doubted that Mephistopheles would bother to ring the bell before showing up uninvited. Ditto for Blackheart and his pals.

He wasn't expecting anybody else.

The elevator door slid open, and Roxanne was standing inside.

Johnny stared at her in shock. She was the last person he had ever expected to find on his doorstep, especially after the emphatic way she had written him off only a few hours ago.

" 'He was right? We can't be together?' "

She was throwing his own words back in his face. "What . . . ?" Johnny still didn't understand what was happening here.

"That's what you said to me," she reminded him. "You said my father was right and that we couldn't be together."

She pushed past Johnny into his apartment.

"Um . . . come on in," was all he managed to get out.

Roxanne paced restlessly back and forth across the loft, dressed casually in a brown leather jacket, white blouse, and blue jeans. A small golden cross hung around her neck. She kept on talking, like she had a lot to get off her mind: "I was thinking about it and . . . you never agreed with my father about anything. Why now?"

Because you'd never believe the truth in a billion years.

"And you said we '*couldn't*' be together," she pointed out. "If you had said, 'we don't belong together,' or that 'we shouldn't be together' . . . well, that would make sense." She shot him a dirty look across the room. "And by the way, I'd totally agree. But 'can't be together' sounds like there's another reason, some outside force making the decision."

Yeah, tell me about it, Johnny thought. "You're reading too much into it."

Roxanne wasn't buying it for a moment. "I said a horrible, cruel, untrue thing to you—for which, by the by, I really apologize—and you . . . you actually *agreed* with me." She shook her head. "I know I haven't seen you in fifteen years, but that's just not you, Johnny."

I'm not me anymore. Just stick around for a while, until the sun goes down.

Unnerved by his silence, she glanced down at the floor. Curiosity showed upon her face as she discovered that she was standing in the middle of Johnny's scattered books and papers. *Wait!* he thought as she reached down and selected a title at random. Just his luck, she picked up *The Rise of the Midnight Son*. He cringed inside as she flipped the book open to the drawing of the End of Days. *How am I going to explain this one?*

She frowned at the illustration, obviously troubled by the disturbing image and subject matter. Concern showed in her eyes as she looked up at Johnny.

"What's going on?" she asked.

Johnny stepped forward and plucked the book from her hand. He started cleaning up the floor around her, sticking the loose pile of torn pages into the nearest convenient drawer. With an air of finality, he slammed the drawer shut.

"We're not the same people we were back then," he

said, knowing full well just how lame that sounded. He piled the satanic tomes back behind Grace. "That's all I was trying to say."

He then walked over to the kitchen. "Want a drink?"

"No," Roxanne said flatly. She strolled over to the unlit fireplace, where a strip of black-and-white snapshots, the kind typically found at a carnival photo booth, occupied a position on honor on the mantel. Her voice softened. "I remember that day."

She turned to watch Johnny pour jelly beans into a martini glass. She raised an eyebrow at the unusual "cocktail."

"I don't drink," Johnny said with a shrug. "Nightmares."

He said it casually enough, but she picked up on the word right away. "Nightmares . . . ?"

"Look, Roxanne," he mumbled, trying desperately to change the subject. "I know I've been acting strange and . . . I'm sorry about dinner, about all of it. Chasing you down on the highway, standing you up again . . ."

"*Are you okay?*" she asked him intensely. She didn't sound mad at all anymore, just worried. About him.

Johnny paused, at a loss for what to say. He couldn't lie to Roxanne. She knew him too well. Always had.

But there was nothing she could do to save him. His fate had been decided fifteen years ago, in a maintenance tent outside Sweetwater.

"I'm fine," he said finally.

"You don't seem fine," she insisted. Here now was the persistence that had made her a top investigative journalist. "You seem anything but fine. Talk to me. Whatever it is, you can trust me."

Could he really? He stared into her deep chestnut eyes, wanting so much to open up to her, but afraid to reveal the unholy shame that had haunted him all these years. Aside from his recent run-in with Caretaker, he had never spoken of his curse with another living soul, let alone a woman he truly cared about.

She saw the hesitation in his eyes. "Tell me the truth, Johnny."

"You wouldn't believe me," he warned her. "*I wouldn't believe me.*"

She plopped down on the couch and patted the seat beside her. "Try me."

"You'll think I'm crazy," he said, reluctantly joining her on the couch. Was he actually thinking of doing this?

"In my job, I've seen and heard just about everything," she assured him. "Twice. There's nothing you can say that would surprise me."

Okay, you asked for it.

"I made a deal with the Devil," Johnny said.

She blinked at him, stunned into momentary silence. Whatever she had been expecting to hear—that he was gay, that there was another woman, that he was an addict, that he was deeply in debt to the Mafia, whatever—the real truth had not been on her radar. To her credit, though, she kept a mostly straight face, only sneaking a quick glance back at the heap of occult volumes stacked behind Grace. She nodded slowly, encouraging him to continue.

"That's why I left you at that tree," he explained, "to spare you."

"Spare me from what?"

"From what happened last night. He came to collect on the deal." She looked confused, so he spelled it out for her, growing agitated. "The Devil. Mephistopheles. And now I work for him and he's got me chasing this guy named Blackheart. And these other guys who change shape. That's why I missed our dinner."

Oh man, this is not going well.

"Because you were at work," she repeated. "For the Devil."

He nodded. "I'm his bounty hunter. The Ghost Rider. Only when I hunt, I don't look like this. I change. So does Grace. We're on fire . . . literally. And when the sun comes up, I change back. Caretaker explained it to me."

"Caretaker?"

"This guy I met," Johnny attempted to explain. "Kind of an old cowboy . . . works at this cemetery. He seems to know a lot about all this, but I'm not sure how."

Roxanne glanced at the clock on the wall. Sunset was upon them. "So tonight, you'll . . ." She curled her hand into a claw and did her best werewolf impression. ". . . arrrgh?"

"I believe so," he told her.

She seemed to need a moment to process what she had just heard. They stared at each other in silence for the space of a heartbeat. Was she giving him the benefit of the doubt? Then she shook her head sadly. A bitter chuckle escaped her lips. "And that's your excuse for fifteen years ago, for last night, for everything?"

"Yeah," he admitted. What else could he say?

"Okay . . ." she started, anger smoldering on her face. "The way I see it, I've got a couple choices here. One, I accept that you really believe that what you just told me is true and I take you to the nearest psychiatric hospital. Or two, I accept that you'd rather make up ridiculous stories than be honest with me . . . and I walk out that door forever."

Neither option sounded very appealing. *Or you could just believe me.* But that was probably asking too much.

The tension in the air was growing thicker by the second. Johnny waited to see what Roxanne's next move would be.

She got off the couch and headed for the door.

Of course. What did you expect? he told himself.

Crushed and defeated, he followed her down to the street and watched ruefully as she opened the door to her car. For once, her cameraman was nowhere around. Roxanne paused before getting into the driver's seat, turning around to take one last look at the dejected man standing on the curb. Her moist brown eyes held a trace of regret.

"Take care of yourself, Johnny," she said softly. "I mean that."

She got in the car and drove away. He watched her taillights disappear around the corner.

Twilight was already falling over the city. It probably wouldn't be long now before Ghost Rider hit the streets again.

God, he was already accepting this insanity as par for the course.

Maybe it's better this way then, he told himself. Roxanne deserved more than to waste her love on a soul doomed to eternal damnation. He hoped she could find someone else, someone who could make her happy.

Someone who isn't cursed.

"Johnny Blaze?"

A gray-haired man stepped out of a nearby alley. He held up a badge. "Captain Dolan," he identified himself. "Fort Worth Police."

What the hell . . . ? "There some kind of problem?"

"Yeah, you could say that," Dolan answered.

Two black-and-white police cars zoomed up to the curb. A bunch of uniformed cops hurried out of the cars—guns drawn and pointed at Johnny. He lifted his hands in confusion.

Metal cuffs jangled in a burly officer's grip. "Take his bike to Impound," Dolan ordered. One of the cops headed for the elevator.

Grace? They want Grace, too? What the hell was happening? What did the police want with him?

He suddenly imagined his mug shot being splashed all over the nightly news. The tabloids would have a field day with this, but that was the least of Johnny's concerns right now.

What happens when the sun goes down?

The cuffs clicked shut around his wrists.

13

St. Michael's Church was closed for the evening. Father Anthony Isabella locked the front doors and took a final tour of the building before retiring for the night. He walked down the center aisle past rows of empty pews. The dying sunlight filtered through the stained-glass windows overlooking the interior of the cathedral. Red votive candles glowed brightly upon the altar. Bouquets of fresh flowers adorned the sanctuary. A scent of incense hung in the air. Everything seemed to be in order. He crossed himself as he approached the altar.

"Forgive me, Father, for I have sinned."

A voice behind him caught the priest by surprise. Turning around, he discovered a young man in a black suit standing only a few steps away. Wicked amusement glinted in the youth's dark eyes. He smirked at the older man's shocked expression.

"I've sinned a lot."

A rustling sound came from an alcove to the right. Water dripped loudly somewhere to the left. Looking around hastily, Father Isabella saw two more figures lurking at both ends of the transept. Greasy dreadlocks blew about the pale face of one of the intruders. Long damp hair concealed the features of the other.

Lord preserve me, the frightened priest thought. He sensed instinctively that he was in the presence of genuine Evil. He held up his cross and rosary. *Satan, get thee behind me!*

The black-garbed youth slapped the holy objects out of Father Isabella's hands. The crucifix clattered against the marble floor. The rosary came apart, spilling beads in all directions. Aghast, the priest stared at the fallen items that had failed to protect him from his enemies. Why had the Lord forsaken him? Was his faith not strong enough?

The youth lunged forward and seized Father Isabella by the throat. "I am searching for a grave," he informed his captive. "One that used to be buried where the old train station is now. Your church relocated the graves."

"I don't know what you're talking about," the priest gulped. He felt duty-bound not to further this foul being's purposes, whatever they might be. Perhaps if he feigned ignorance, this evil would pass him by. . . .

The youth's grip tightened around his throat, so that Father Isabella could barely breathe. "Oh, I think you do," he said. "In fact, I can feel you thinking about it right now. . . ."

The priest gasped for breath as the youth's black eyes seemed to bore into his very soul. The youth's pale face took on a demonic cast. White teeth sharpened into fangs. All thought of resistance evaporated from Father Isabella's mind, replaced by an overwhelming desire to save his own skin. *Forgive me, Lord,* he prayed. *Forgive my pitiable human weakness.*

"There . . . are records," he admitted.

Trembling, Father Isabella led the youth and his two unnatural companions down to the church basement. Dust and cobwebs suggested that no one had poked around in the old records for years. Mice scurried away at their approach. His shaking hand extracted a leather-bound volume from a shelf. He cracked the book open, raising a cloud of dust that left him coughing for a spell. Inside the volume, handwritten notations filled the yellow pages. He scanned the pages, but could make no sense of the entries.

"These are the records," he volunteered, "but . . . I don't read Latin."

"A dead language," the youth conceded. He plucked the volume from Father Isabella's hands and began leafing through the pages. He seemed to have no difficulty deciphering the scrawled notations. Lifting his eyes from the pages, he noted the priest's puzzled expression.

"Private school," he explained.

"Those things will kill you," Captain Dolan remarked.

Johnny lit up the cigarette anyway. "They'll have to get in line. . . ."

He had never been in a police interrogation room before, but Johnny recognized the decor from countless TV cop shows. He sat behind a cheap pine table, staring into a long horizontal mirror that was undoubtedly a one-way window. The bare concrete walls were painted institutional green. An ashtray rested on the table before him. The legs of his chair scraped against the scuffed tile floor.

"Act like a tough guy, fine." Dolan faced him across the table. A younger officer, Edwards, slid a folder toward Johnny. Inside were a series of photographs. Johnny glimpsed several shots of torn-up blacktop and a close-up of a mangled license plate. *So that's how they got me,* he realized. He hadn't even noticed the plate was missing. *Guess I had other things on my mind.*

Dolan ran down the evidence against him. "Your plate and a tread from your tires at the crime scene. A witness that will testify that the suspect used some kind of *fire* effect. Like the ones you use in your stunt shows."

"I told you," Johnny insisted. "I don't know anything."

Anything you'll believe, that is, you idiot.

Dolan ran out of patience. He grabbed Johnny by the collar and forced him to look at another photo in the file. This one showed a mummified corpse that appeared to have been dyed an unnatural shade of blue. The body wore the tattered remains of a stationmaster's uniform. Bifocals perched on the mummy's indigo nose.

"This guy was three years from retirement," Dolan

informed him. "Never harmed a fly. And take a look at some of the other corpses that have turned up since you came home." He spread the photos out in front of Johnny, confronting his prisoner with shot after shot of withered corpses. Taut blue flesh stretched over the grotesque blue cadavers, who looked like they'd had the very life sucked out of them.

Johnny stared at the pictures, unable to look away. For one horrible moment, he wondered if maybe the Ghost Rider *was* responsible for the killings. *Did I do this?*

No. The stationmaster's body had already been lying at Blackheart's feet when the Ghost Rider had arrived at the depot.

"I didn't kill anyone," he murmured, as much to himself as to the cops. *Except maybe that one freaky demon, the one who drove the truck into me.* A vivid memory, of the earth elemental being reduced to shards by Ghost Rider's fiery chain, flashed through his mind. *Is incinerating a demon a crime? Maybe not on this earth.*

"Maybe not," Dolan said. "But I'm guessing you can tell me who did." He let go of Johnny's collar. "We *know* the crimes scenes are connected. Forensics confirms it, they all died the same way. The old guy at the depot and the ones at the biker bar."

Biker bar? Johnny recalled hearing something about some sort of massacre on the news. Had Blackheart been responsible for that tragedy as well? What was he up to anyway? Why did Mephistopheles want the rebellious demon and his buddies dragged back to Hell? Johnny tried to fit the pieces together in his mind. He wondered how much Caretaker knew about what was really going on.

Not that Dolan seemed inclined to let Johnny go anytime soon. "The famous Johnny Blaze," the cop said mockingly, letting the prisoner know that his celebrity status wasn't going to do him any good here. "Seems to me that your fans wouldn't be too keen on you being wrapped up in a murder investigation. Not to mention corporate sponsors, event promoters . . ."

Detective Edwards nodded along with his boss, looking like he expected Johnny to crack under the pressure. But Johnny couldn't care less about the policemen's threats. *The Devil owns my soul*, he thought mordantly. *Yeah, like I'm really worried about my ticket sales and product endorsements.*

He leaned back in his chair and crossed his arms atop his chest. There was nothing the cops could do to him that could match the bottomless pit he had already dug for himself. This was just a sideshow.

"So," Dolan growled, "you wanna talk? Or do you wanna spend the night in the tank?"

Johnny took another drag on his cigarette.

Moments later, he was being roughly escorted by armed officers toward a holding cell enclosed by sturdy iron bars. Over a dozen inmates—a pretty unsavory-looking crowd—glared at him from beneath the sickly fluorescent lights. Prison tattoos and surly scowls advertised anti-social tendencies. Old scars hinted at past brawls and gang wars. Clenched fists promised more violence to come.

Caretaker's words echoed inside Johnny's skull. *"At night, in the presence of evil . . ."*

Johnny glanced at a clock on the wall. Night would be falling soon, if it hadn't already.

He saw a very bad situation developing.

"You *don't* want to put me in there," he warned the guards.

"Sorry," one of the cops replied. "The Ritz was booked."

His colleague opened the door to the cell and shoved Johnny inside. The door slammed shut, locking Johnny in with the other prisoners. Ugly smiles, whistles, and catcalls welcomed him.

"Hey!" a six-foot-tall skinhead snarled at him. Wearing a studded leather jacket, the punk elbowed his way through the crowd toward Johnny. "You look like that Johnny Blaze dude. . . ."

Great, Johnny thought. *Another fan.* He didn't feel like signing autographs right now. "Yeah. I get that a lot."

"Nah, that *is* you!" the skinhead insisted. "You're him! I saw you jump at that state fair a few years ago." He scowled at the memory. "I paid ten bucks to see you splatter. But you didn't."

"Sorry to disappoint you," Johnny said.

A hefty redneck wearing faded military fatigues

lumbered up to him. A Confederate flag adorned his black baseball cap. "You might be a big shot out there, Blaze," he jeered. He cracked his knuckles ominously. "But in here, you're just another monkey in the cage."

"I'm not looking for any trouble," Johnny said. Was there any way to keep this scene from escalating out of control?

The redneck snorted. "Looks like trouble found you." Without warning, he rammed his fist into Johnny's stomach. The pain was immediate, intense, and Johnny doubled over. The skinhead grabbed onto Johnny and spun him around—the better to peel his leather jacket away from him.

"Nice jacket," he chortled.

A slim teenage African-American nervously stepped forward, looking extremely out of place among the other inmates. Sensitive features betrayed his discomfort at the brutal treatment Johnny was receiving.

"C'mon, man," he pleaded. "Leave him alone."

"Get lost!" the skinhead barked. He backhanded the guy across the mouth, sending him flying across the cell. The other prisoners practically trampled over the poor kid in their rush to join in beating up the legendary Johnny Blaze. Punks, bikers, and gangbangers fell upon Johnny like a pack of wolves tearing apart a wounded deer. Fists and boots collided with Johnny's tender flesh, knocking him to the floor. His face was pounded into the cement. He felt the stitches in his shoulder come loose. Fresh blood dripped down his arm.

"I get his boots!" the redneck bellowed.

"Gimme that watch!" another prisoner shouted.

"Goddamn pretty boy!" a shaggy Hell's Angel cursed. The rockers on his vest proclaimed his outlaw status. Symbolic patches bragged of past crimes and sex acts. "Calls himself a biker . . ."

"Let go of that jacket! I saw it first!"

Johnny disappeared beneath a pile of thrashing criminals.

Then all hell broke loose.

The transformation caught everyone off-guard.

One moment, they were all gleefully beating the famous Johnny Blaze to a pulp. The next, an eerie orange glow emanated from beneath the heap of bodies, followed by a blinding burst of white-hot fire that blasted the inmates into the walls of the cell. Iron bars rang like tuning forks. Spots appeared before the eyes of onlooking prisoners.

Ghost Rider rose from the floor, a nimbus of crackling yellow flames surrounding his grinning skull.

The flames set off the sprinkler system, but the spraying water failed to douse the Rider's fiery aura. His blazing sockets spotted the skinhead lying on the floor nearby. The bald hoodlum's face had been baked red by Ghost Rider's volcanic transmutation. He looked like he was suffering from the world's worst case of sunburn. The rest of the inmates looked toasted as well.

"Oh, hell," the skinhead fearfully murmured. A skeletal hand closed around the punk's throat, the mystic flames licking against his skin, as Ghost Rider effortlessly lifted him off the floor. The skinhead yowled in pain as his feet dangled in the air. He tugged at the bony claw with both hands, but was unable to pry the burning fingers away from his neck. Ghost Rider looked him over without mercy.

"*Nice jacket,*" he intoned.

Johnny's own jacket lay crumpled on the floor, torn by the greedy hands of competing felons, so Ghost Rider claimed the skinhead's jacket as his own. Metal studs popped as he pulled the jacket over his skeletal frame, adapting it to his use. Shining silver spikes rose from the jacket's shoulders, giving the Rider an even more forbidding look. Bad to the bone, in more ways than one.

The flaming skull surveyed the crowded cell, as the terrified inmates backed away from the hellish apparition that had suddenly appeared in their midst.

They were trapped inside the cell with Ghost Rider, with no way to escape his stern and unforgiving justice.

"*Guilty,*" he pronounced. His unforgiving gaze swept from face to face. "*Guilty. Guilty. Guilty. . . .*"

Only a few yards away, a bored guard whiled away the hours in the surveillance room. His heels rested on the electronic control panel in front of him. Closed-circuit television screens kept watch over the precinct house, but the guard's eyes were glued to the PlayStation Portable in his lap. His thumbs worked the controls as he tried to break his record on *Johnny Blaze—Airtime!* On the handheld game's display screen, the CG biker crashed and burned for the umpteenth time.

"*And Blaze is down!*" the game announced.

The guard groaned. "This game is impossible." He tossed the console onto the control panel, then gave the various screens a cursory glance. After all, that's what they paid him for. . . .

The fire alarm went off.

He sat up straight in his chair, dropping his feet back down onto the floor. His eyes bugged out as he took a closer look at the monitors. "Holy crap!"

In the holding cell, a skull-headed biker was summarily kicking the asses of over a dozen hardened criminals.

A brilliant yellow flame encircled the skeleton's cranium. Savage spikes jutted from his gloves and shoulders. He tossed the terrified perps around like they were rag dolls. Flying bodies crashed into clots of hysterical inmates, who were practically climbing the walls to get away from the fearsome biker. The spray from the sprinklers flooded the floor of the cell, causing the prisoners to slip and fall. Cold water sluiced down the biker's black leather gear, which dried almost instantaneously. Steam rose from his head and shoulders. Steel-toed boots splashed through the spreading pool beneath him. Bony fists clobbered the other prisoners.

The cop rubbed his eyes, but the incredible images didn't go away. His hand dropped instinctively onto the grip of his baton. Who—or what—did they have in that cell?

He hit the panic button.

The impound garage was packed with confiscated vehicles, in various states of disrepair. Deputy Gary Friedrich worked his way through the crowded garage, filling out evidence reports on his clipboard. He fought back a yawn. One of these days he really was going to put in for a transfer to the day shift. Working nights sucked.

A vintage Harley-Davidson occupied a formerly empty slot. Friedrich whistled in appreciation of the fine-looking machine. He wouldn't mind taking a spin on that chopper. He walked toward the bike, checking it against the description on the original report. His interest in the bike increased when he read that it belonged to Johnny Blaze, the famous daredevil. He had caught Blaze's show at the stadium the other day—that *had* been a pretty impressive stunt with all those helicopters.

He wondered what Blaze was in for. *Probably drugs or DUI*, he guessed. That was usually what got celebrities into trouble. *Too much money and free time.*

A sudden roar from the Harley's engine caused him to nearly jump out of his skin. The enclosed garage amplified the echo of the engine's furious growl, creating an almost deafening racket. "What the hell?"

Before his eyes, Blaze's bike burst into flames. The metal chassis writhed like a thing alive, taking on a more satanic design. A skull-like visage emerged from the fairings. The wheels ignited, turning into spinning rings of fire. Friedrich tumbled backward onto his butt. He threw his hands up in front of his face, just in case the gas tank exploded. The transformed cycle shifted loudly into gear, like it was about to run him over. There was no chance that he could get out of the way in time.

Instead the riderless bike launched itself into the air, sailing over the sprawled deputy and touching down on the pavement behind him. Flames spewed from its exhaust pipes as it zoomed for the exit. A trail of molten asphalt marked its passage.

That's it, Friedrich thought, pale-faced and sweating. *I'm* definitely *transferring to days!*

Twitching bodies littered the floor of the cell. Even the worst among the inmates had proven no match for Ghost Rider's vengeful fists and Penance Stare. Of all the prisoners, only the fragile teenager remained upon his feet. He cowered in the far corner of the cell, watching the Rider with undisguised dread. The skinhead's blow had left an ugly purple bruise upon his cheek.

"*You*," Ghost Rider addressed him. He pointed a bony finger at the frightened young man. "*Innocent*."

He turned away from the kid and kicked open the cell door. The steel bars clanged against the floor as he strode out of the cell and down the hallway beyond. Unable to believe his good fortune, the teenager watched the Spirit of Vengeance depart, then fainted dead away onto the floor.

The Hellcycle was waiting for Ghost Rider as he marched out the back exit of the precinct house. Across a narrow strip of pavement, a lighted red sign spelled out GARAGE above the entrance to the impound. A flaming trail stretched down the ramp to where the Hellcycle now stood.

"Hold it!"

The surveillance guard charged up and cracked the flaming skull in the face with his baton. Ghost Rider turned to look at his attacker. The guard gulped as he saw that the skull's lower jaw had come unhinged; the bony mandible hung loosely to one side. Yellow flames rippled along the dislocated jaw.

That's no mask, the guard realized. He felt sick to his stomach.

Ghost Rider casually reached up and reset his jaw. It clicked back into place. He waved his finger in the guard's face, chiding him for his rash move.

The guard swallowed hard. "My bad."

Ghost Rider climbed onto the Hellcycle. He peeled away from the police station in a torrid burst of flame. Hellfire flared from the rear of the bike, shattering the first three letters of the garage sign.

Only the word RAGE remained intact, glowing brightly like a warning to the wicked.

Vengeance rode the streets of the city.

14

An armada of police cruisers pursued Ghost Rider along the waterfront. The Hellcycle split the lanes, zooming between rows of civilian cars and trucks. Shocked drivers stared in fear and amazement as the skeletal biker sped past them, leaving a trail of fire right down the middle of the drive. Wailing police sirens disturbed the night. Law-abiding Texans pulled their own vehicles to the side to let the fleet of flashing cop cars through. Police helicopters joined in the pursuit, racing to keep up with the flaming chopper. Airborne searchlights targeted the Hellcycle. Amplified voices called on Ghost Rider to stop and surrender.

But the Spirit of Vengeance answered to no earthly authority. He didn't even look up at the helicopters, let alone slow down. Intent upon his mission, he would let nothing come between him and his foes. If he could just elude these troublesome mortals, he might be able to pick up Blackheart's trail again.

The west fork of the Trinity River flowed sluggishly along the right side of the roadway. Pedestrians strolling the riverfront yelped and dived for cover. Braver citizens grabbed for their cameras and cell phones, hoping to catching a picture of the high-speed chase. Dogs on leashes barked wildly at the spectral biker.

Up ahead, a railroad bridge crossed the river. Hoping to shake his pursuers, Ghost Rider took a sharp turn onto the bridge. He leaned into the curve, scraping the bike against the tarmac. Flaming wheels rode the rails, emitting a shower of sparks, until Ghost Rider spotted the police road block waiting for him on the other side. He hit the brakes, halting in the middle of the bridge. SWAT teams took up positions at both ends of the iron trestle. Wooden barricades and throngs of parked police cars added to the blockades. Helicopters whirred overhead. Hundreds of feet below him, the moonlit surface of the river rippled slowly.

We've got him now, Captain Dolan thought. He slammed a fist into his palm in satisfaction. Blaze was trapped upon the bridge, with nowhere to go. Dolan couldn't wait to rip that freaky mask off the daredevil's head. He still couldn't figure out how Blaze had escaped from jail in the first place. *No way is he getting away from us again!*

Standing behind a blue wooden sawhorse, he gave the SWAT teams the go-ahead. He didn't bother trying to talk Blaze off the bridge; the berserk celebrity had already had plenty of chances to surrender willingly. "Go get him!" he barked into his walkie-talkie. "I want that biker's skull!"

The SWAT teams, wearing fireproof body armor, converged on the flaming apparition from both sides. Dolan waited to see if Blaze would be stupid enough, or crazy enough, to put up a fight.

But Ghost Rider took another route.

He swung the front wheels of the chopper toward the edge of bridge, gunned his engine, and *drove right over the brink.* Dolan watched in shock as the blazing cycle plunged over two hundred feet into the river below. The bike hit the water with an enormous splash, then disappeared beneath the surface. Steaming ripples spread out across the river from the point of impact.

That crazy idiot! Dolan thought angrily. *He killed himself!*

The twin SWAT teams ran out onto the bridge, then peered over the edge at the unsettled water below. Dolan hurried out to join them. Looking down from the bridge, he was surprised to see a dim yellow glow slowly fading beneath the roiling current. "Let's get some nets over here!" he ordered. If they moved quickly, maybe they could still snag onto the biker's body before the river carried it away. He wanted to confirm once and for all that the so-called Ghost Rider was actually Johnny Blaze in disguise.

Shame things had to end this way, he thought. The guy seemed to have everything going for him: wealth, fame, a hot girlfriend. So what had caused him to go berserk all of a sudden? *Suicide is no way to go.*

Before they could even begin dragging the Trinity, however, the river below them suddenly churned and bubbled, like water coming to a boil. A rumbling noise came from somewhere beneath the surface, growing louder by the second. Steam and white water frothed violently atop the river as the Ghost Rider suddenly erupted out of the murky water.

"What—?" Dolan gasped. Beside him, a SWAT team member lifted the visor of his helmet, seemingly unable to believe his eyes. Startled shouts and exclamations sounded all along the bridge as Ghost Rider's flaming cycle, undoused by its immersion beneath the Trinity, zoomed away on *top* of the river . . . like a hydrofoil from Hell. Fiery wheels outraced the current, spewing a trail of eerie blue flames that burned atop the water like a flaming oil slick. Ghost Rider's blazing sockets glanced back briefly at the stupefied police officers upon the bridge. For a second, Dolan felt as if the glowing skull was looking right at him. An amused grin appeared upon the bony visage.

The cycle rocketed away down the river, swiftly leaving the police helicopters behind him. Dolan couldn't even begin to guess how fast the demonic bike was traveling, and over the water, no less. All his theories and suppositions regarding Johnny Blaze's secret life as the Rider went up in smoke. Junior officers turned to him for answers, wanting to know what to do now. Dolan watched the sputtering blue flames slowly die away.

He didn't have a clue.

The unconscious priest was suspended above the basement floor, Blackheart's fingers still tight around his throat. The Devil's son flipped through the old church records with his free hand. He smiled as he perused the pages, realizing that he was nearing the end of his unholy quest. *My hour of ascendance draws nigh*, he thought, *and there is nothing my father can do to stop it.*

Satisfied that he had read enough, he closed the moldering book and released his grip on Father Isabella, who collapsed onto the bare stone floor. Only the flutter of his eyelids, and a distinct lack of blue pigmentation, testified that the unlucky priest was still alive. Eager to attain his ultimate goal, Blackheart was in too much of a hurry to dispose of the priest properly.

"I have everything I need," he informed his remaining followers. Abigor and Wallow lingered in the shadows of the basement, awaiting Blackheart's next command. The muffled sounds of wind and water betrayed their presence.

The unmistakable roar of a motorcycle penetrated the basement walls, coming from outside the church. The sound grew louder by the second.

The Rider.

"He's coming for us!" Wallow gurgled. Anxiety literally dripped from his face.

Blackheart was less alarmed by the Rider's approach. He had never imagined that his father's bloodhound would not track them down again. One way or another, the Rider needed to be dealt with.

"Abigor."

The air elemental whipped his head around, his features a blur of motion. The breezes blowing his dreadlocks about increased in intensity. He looked to Blackheart for his marching orders.

"You know what to do," his leader said.

Ghost Rider raced down the street, drawn by the stench of the hellborn evil at large tonight. Drivers and pedestrians alike fled from the sight of the avenging spirit on his incendiary chopper. He screeched to a halt in front of a Catholic church wedged in between several of downtown's larger buildings. He listened intently to the sounds of the night, straining all his senses in order to zero in on his prey. His chain was slung across his chest. Spiked gauntlets, found in the pockets of his "borrowed" jacket, encased his hands. He looked up and down the street in front of the church.

I'm close, he realized. *They're somewhere nearby*.

He peered up at the upper floors of the church. Something fluttered in the breeze above the parapet. Stone gargoyles leered at him from the base of the steeple. Ghost Rider sensed that they were not alone.

A tremendous blast of wind blew him off his cycle. He cartwheeled backward into a parked car, denting it deeply in one side and shattering the passenger-side windows. His flaming aura scorched the paint off the car.

A swirling cloud of dirty air gusted from the church steeple to the roof of a two-story office building across the street. Abigor howled at Ghost Rider from his vantage point high above the street.

"Call off the hunt, Rider!"

Never! Ghost Rider thought. Extricating himself from the crumpled car, he mounted his Hellcycle once more and rode toward the office building. A boarded-up newsstand burst into flame.

But Abigor did not stay in one place very long. His corporeal form dissolved into an insubstantial mist as he blew across the sky toward a looming glass-and-steel skyscraper a few blocks away. Revving his engine, Ghost Rider chased after the fugitive demon, but not even the Hellcycle could outrun the wind. Abigor blasted himself to the top of the skyscraper, then rematerialized upon the ledge. His demonic laughter carried across the distance as he crouched at the edge of the rooftop, beckoning for the Rider to follow him up to where he had the advantage. "Come and get me!" he taunted, capering upon the ledge. "If you dare!"

Ghost Rider's flames heated up, growing bright enough to light up the darkness. Snarling, he poured his power into the Hellcycle's infernal engine, accelerating toward the skyscraper at breakneck speed. Anger blazed in his eye sockets.

The vile elemental would elude his judgment no longer.

Burning tires tore up the street.

Officer Howard Mackie was behind the wheel of his patrol car when the flaming motorcycle zipped by him. The bizarre sight matched the APBs he'd received earlier regarding a biker in a glow-in-the-dark Halloween mask riding a burning chopper. He had briefly wondered whether the gang in Dispatch had been pulling his leg, but seeing was believing. Fire crackled around the bony skull of the biker up ahead as he veered around the corner into a maze of narrow alleyways.

"Mackie to Base! Mackie to Base!" he yelped into his mike. "I have a suspect fleeing west on Cherry. Repeat, west on Cherry. Suspect matches the description of the fugitive who broke out of the precinct house. . . ."

Activating his lights and sirens, he took off in pursuit of the flaming bike. He stared in confusion at the chopper's blazing wheels. *How does that work?* he wondered, trying to figure out what kind of fuel the biker might have doused the tires with. *Why doesn't the rubber melt?*

"That's a dead end," headquarters reported back. "You got him."

"10-4 on that!" Mackie replied. *Looks like I'm going to get a chance to check out those trick wheels firsthand.*

Sure enough, a towering steel skyscraper loomed directly in the motorcycle's path, blocking any possible escape route. Stone steps led up from an enclosed plaza to the front of the building. Banners, affixed to the stone columns flanking the steps, advertised the city's daily longhorn cattle drives. The skull-faced biker had nowhere to go. Mackie turned the wailing police car sideways to keep the chopper from pulling a U-turn and heading back out of the alley. He hit the brakes and reached for his service pistol. In theory, the biker wasn't supposed to be armed, but he wasn't taking any chances.

End of the road, cowboy.

He stepped out of his car in time to see the motor-cycle reach the base of the skyscraper—and ride straight up the side of the seventy-five story building.

Mackie's jaw dropped. His arms fell limply to his sides.

A voice from his police radio asked for an update. "What is the suspect's 10-20?"

His gaze still locked on the ascending cycle, he pulled the mike toward him.

"Up," he reported flatly.

Dispatch sounded understandably puzzled. "What?"

"The suspect is going *up*!"

On the fourteenth floor of the Plaza Hotel, Roxanne was packing her bags. She had a return flight in the morning, which was not nearly soon enough as far as she was concerned. She couldn't wait to leave the Dallas-Forth Worth area and get back to her home territory in Atlanta, where hopefully she would never have to deal with Johnny Blaze again. Her "brilliant" idea to interview the elusive daredevil had only succeeded in breaking her heart all over again.

Did he really expect me to believe that he was in thrall to the Devil? She shook her head, remembering that insane encounter in Johnny's loft. *How gullible did he think I was?* She angrily folded a spare outfit and stuffed it into her suitcase. *Oh well*, she consoled herself, *at least I got to cover a couple of juicy stories while I was out here.*

Her bags were spread out atop the queen-sized bed. She turned away from the bed to retrieve some items from the closet when her gaze was caught by a trail of fire streaking up the side of the skyscraper across the street. She stared in amazement, not entirely grasping what she was seeing at first. Was that actually a *motorcycle* defying gravity as it headed up the building at a ninety-degree angle to the street? Panes of glass exploded in the chopper's wake, raining down on the sidewalk below.

She instantly thought of Johnny—and what he claimed would happen to him when the sun went down:

"We're on fire . . . literally."

Her jaw hanging open, she watched the blazing cycle climb the building like a bat out of hell. Who else could pull off a stunt like that . . .

. . . except maybe the Devil's bounty hunter?

"Oh my God," she whispered.

The top of the skyscraper was right in front of him. Ghost Rider launched the Hellcycle over the ledge and arced through the air before touching down on the rooftop. Tar paper ignited upon contact with his wheels. The throbbing engine idled beneath him as he scanned the area for his foe. Ventilation fans whirred upon the roof, alongside wireless antennae and satellite dishes, but Abigor was nowhere to be seen.

A cyclonic blast of wind struck the Rider, sending him skidding across the roof toward the waiting precipice. Fighting back against the wind, he dug in his heels and stopped himself only inches from the ledge. He clenched his fists as Abigor materialized only a few paces away.

"You should have joined us, Rider," the elemental taunted. His hair and clothing flapped about in a perpetual whirlwind. He stroked his greasy goatee. "Now you'll only be a footnote in the history of New Hell."

Ghost Rider glowered at the demon. *"Where is Blackheart?"*

Abigor laughed in his face. "Blackheart is the Beast," he boasted. "And he's here to create Hell on Earth!" He dissipated into the air, vanishing from sight.

Ghost Rider spun around in search of the demon, only to be knocked off his feet by an overpowering gust of wind. Abigor floated up from the rooftop, rising over twenty feet in the air. Storm winds gathered around him, howling like the damned. Smog rushed in from all over the city, soiling the very air. He threw out his arms, summoning all his elemental power for one final assault. The tail of a whirlwind lashed the rooftop below.

Roxanne burst from the front entrance of the Plaza. She raced across the street, heedless of the oncoming traffic. Horns honked and brakes squealed, but she paid them no mind. All her attention was on the ravaged skyscraper up ahead. She looked intently at the top of the building, but couldn't see the Ghost Rider any-more, only a trail of broken windows leading up to the rooftop. A sulfurous odor hung in the air.

Like brimstone, she remembered. Could Johnny have killed all those people? *I just don't know anymore.*

A police car was parked at the base of the skyscraper. A dazed-looking cop tried to wave her away, but she ran right past him. Shattered glass crunched beneath her heels as she ran up the steps to the building. Melted asphalt clung to her soles. She tugged on the front door, only to find it locked for the night. Her fists pounded against the unyielding glass and steel.

Somebody let me in!

The concerned cop gently pulled her away from the building. She stared bleakly at the skyscraper's daunting heights. She would have given anything to know what was happening up on the roof. Her whole world de-pended on it.

"Johnny!"

• • •

Atop the roof, Ghost Rider faced off against Abigor.

The elemental hovered in the air above the earthbound Rider. Whirling winds whipped up the dust and soot around Ghost Rider's feet, as well as the flames encircling his skull. The fires flickered weakly in the wind, like a candle on the verge of being blown out.

"You're a slow learner, aren't you?" Abigor mocked him. "You can't catch the wind, Rider!"

"Wrong!" Ghost Rider declared. Uncoiling the chain around his chest, he infused the adamantine links with hellfire. He spun the chain before him, creating a whirling ring of fire. Bright orange flames blurred into a fiery loop.

"What . . . ?" Abigor blurted, as he felt a sudden suction pulling at his immaterial form. The spinning chain generated a powerful back draft that drew the demon downward. Realizing his danger, he tried to flee into the cloudy Texas sky, but the pull from the whirling flames was too strong. Against his will, he was dragged back toward the circle of fire. "No!" he howled.

Ghost Rider whirled the chain faster and faster, turning up the heat and intensity. The voracious back draft sucked Abigor into the consuming flames. Hellfire engulfed the screaming elemental, immolating him on the spot. Abigor turned into a churning pillar of ashes that quickly flared out and disappeared.

The winds buffeting Ghost Rider fell still. A handful

of ashes drifted down onto the rooftop. No breeze remained to blow them away.

Vengeance is mine, Ghost Rider thought, but the hunt had barely begun. Blackheart, as well as the last of the Hidden, still awaited his judgment. And many hours remained until dawn. His chain cooled down and he wrapped it back across his chest. *Let the wicked beware*.

Ghost Rider saddled up and rode the Hellcycle back the way he had come. He shot over the ledge and out into the air, seventy-five stories above the ground. The blazing chain lashed out and caught onto the side of the building, shattering another window in the process. The chain went taut, anchoring the soaring chopper to the skyscraper. Flaming wheels grabbed onto the vertical steel and glass, and the Hellcycle roared straight down the side of the building. Fire gushed from its exhaust pipes as the pavement seemed to come rushing up at the biker at over one hundred miles per hour.

"Oh hell, here he comes again!"

Roxanne heard the cop yell out as he dragged her back toward his car. She looked up to see the flaming chopper careering down the side of the skyscraper, heading straight for the ground. Her heart seemed to surge into her throat. She put her hands over her face, almost afraid to look. Anxious eyes peeked through her fingers.

The motorcycle hit the ground with the force of a

missile. The stone steps exploded into pieces. Sewer covers bounced into the air. The pavement shook beneath her feet, throwing her off-balance. She threw out her arms and braced herself against the side of the police car. The cop swore under his breath.

Ghost Rider didn't even lose his seat on the bike. Landing on the wrecked pavement, only a few yards away, he pumped his fist in exhilaration. Roxanne recognized the move.

Oh my God, Johnny, she thought, gazing at the unearthly apparition before her. *It really is you.*

Which meant that . . . everything he had told her in the loft was . . . true?

Her awestruck eyes stared at the blazing skull, searching for some trace of Johnny's handsome features. Ghost Rider saw her looking at him and turned toward her. Was it just her imagination or did she see a spark of recognition glowing at the core of his empty eye sockets?

The specter acted like he knew her. His mane of fire cooled to a faint blue flame. Getting off his demonic cycle, he walked tentatively toward her, like he was afraid of her reaction. A spiked glove reached out for her; a plaintive expression appeared upon the macabre skull-face. Roxanne suddenly felt like she was starring in some ghoulish version of *Beauty and the Beast*, or perhaps *Death Takes a Holiday*. She took a hesitant step in his direction.

"Johnny . . ."

The poignant moment was shattered by the noisy arrival of the three more police cruisers. The black-and-white vehicles came screeching into the plaza in front of the building. Spinning blue lights and wailing sirens assaulted Roxanne's senses. The cop who was helping her before ran forward and dragged her back toward his car, even as his colleagues piled out of the cruisers with their guns raised. Next a SWAT team arrived on the scene, adding automatic rifles to the mix. Visored helmets and body armor concealed the reinforcements' humanity.

"Let me go!" Roxanne pleaded. Strong hands kept her away from Ghost Rider. "I need to talk to him!" Police marksmen aimed their weapons. Roxanne's face filled with fear. "No!" she shouted, although no one was listening. "Don't shoot!"

Ghost Rider shook what appeared to be an angry fist at the police. A wall of fire erupted between the Rider and the cops, causing the police officers to fall back in retreat. Roxanne felt the scorching heat of the flames against her face. The fiery barrier was at least seven feet tall. The banners on the stone columns went up in a blaze.

Through the flames, she saw Ghost Rider get back onto his uniquely customized chopper. She remembered Johnny saying that Grace transformed as well, but the grotesque cycle before her bore no resemblance to his dad's old Harley-Davidson. A skull, serpents, and sculpted vertebrae gleamed in the hellish light of the flames. She didn't know what looked more terrifying—the Ghost Rider or his ride.

The Devil's bounty hunter took one last look at Roxanne. For an instant, she thought she glimpsed Johnny's familiar eyes staring back at her from the shadowy recesses of the skull's eye sockets. Then he peeled away in a burst of fire, leaving Roxanne and the police officers trapped on the other side of dying flames. The bike smashed through the front door of the skyscraper and out the other side of the building. The sound of smashed glass and furniture echoed across the plaza.

Roxanne watched Ghost Rider disappear. Charred pavement and flooring marked his passage.

Forgive me, Johnny, she thought. *I should have believed you.*

But what was she supposed to do now?

Above the trashed plaza, Blackheart peered down over the ledge at the tableau seventy-five stories below. His dark eyes zeroed in on the woman who had tried to go to the Rider, the one he had so pathetically reached for. The woman he so obviously yearned for.

Blackheart didn't know whether to laugh or vomit.

"And now we know his weakness," he announced to Wallow.

The last of the Hidden was busy scooping up his brother's ashes from the scorched rooftop. He blew gently upon the ashes, setting them free upon the wind.

Then he joined Blackheart at the ledge. Angry waters roiled beneath the surface of his face. The Devil's son knew Wallow would stop at nothing to get his revenge upon the Ghost Rider.

Hold that thought, Blackheart mused.

15

CARETAKER WAS CHOPPING FIREWOOD BACK BEHIND his shack when Johnny Blaze pulled up to the cemetery on his bike. Sunlight exposed the exhausted circles under the younger man's eyes. He looked beat . . . like he had been chasing demons all night.

Not to mention escaping from the police.

"They know who I am," he told Caretaker.

The old-timer put down his axe. "Who's that?"

"*Everybody.*" Johnny parked Grace by the shack. He wearily climbed off the bike. "Don't you watch TV? What's the matter with you?"

Caretaker spit onto the ground. "Told you to stick around."

"Is this ever going to end?" Johnny asked.

"It'll end if you can catch them," Caretaker said.

Makes sense, Johnny thought. *That's what bounty hunters do, I guess.* He examined Caretaker's grizzled face. He couldn't help feeling that the mysterious old-timer knew more than he was letting on.

Well, that's not good enough anymore.

"What's really going on?" he asked.

Caretaker looked away, unwilling to meet Johnny's eyes. He fiddled with his axe, wrestling with some inner dilemma. *Is it that he doesn't trust me?* Johnny wondered. *Is that what this is about?*

"Look," he said. "At least give me the courtesy of telling me what it is I'm fighting for."

Caretaker nodded, like he couldn't argue with that logic. He turned back toward Johnny, looking him squarely in the eyes, and seemed to make up his mind.

"Come with me."

He led Johnny to a weathered tombstone not far from the shack. A knotty old hickory stretched its skeletal branches above the grave. Johnny had to strain to read the faded inscription. " 'Carter Slade'?"

"Legend has it," Caretaker said gravely, "that he started out a Texas Ranger, a man of honor. But he got greedy and found himself locked up, waitin' on the gallows. Then the stranger came, offering freedom from the noose. Slade made the deal . . . and ended up as a Phantom Rider."

I can relate. But according to the tombstone, Slade had died nearly one-hundred-and-fifty years ago. "What's he got to do with this?"

"Remember the contract the stranger made with the people of San Venganza?" Caretaker stood a few feet back from the grave site. "The story goes that Slade was sent there to collect the souls, but what he found was so evil that he took the contract and rode off."

"He stole it?" Johnny asked. He wondered what had ever become of that rolled-up parchment he had bled on fifteen years ago. *If only I could steal that one back . . . !*

Caretaker nodded. "To keep Mephistopheles from getting his hands on it again. A thousand evil souls can start a helluva war." He tipped his hat at Carter Slade's grave. "Some people believe he was buried with it."

"Was he?" Johnny asked.

The old-timer thought about it for a moment. "I dunno," he said finally. "But what I do know is that Blackheart's coming for it. And he'll do anything to get it. To anybody." He didn't mince words, giving Johnny the hard truth straight up. "That's why you have to stay away from friends, family, anyone that he could use against you."

"Roxanne," Johnny whispered. He remembered meeting her as Ghost Rider the night before, right after his battle with that air elemental. A terrifying thought chilled him to the marrow. What if Blackheart or his other minion had been lurking around afterward?

They might have seen us together.

He ran to Grace and fired up her engine. The Harley took off at top speed, throwing up a spray of gravel behind her. There was no time to explain to Caretaker. Johnny knew in his heart that Roxanne was in danger . . . because of him.

This is all my fault, he thought. A hot wind blew against his face as he pushed Grace to her limits and beyond. The old cemetery receded behind as he tore toward the city. *I have to warn her!*

Roxanne glanced up at the darkening sky as she walked briskly toward Johnny's apartment. Despite a day's work reviewing her notes and videotapes, she was no closer to finding out where he had vanished to. Meanwhile, the media was having a field day with his arrest and mysterious escape. A newspaper headline screamed at her from a sidewalk stand: CELEBRITY DAREDEVIL ELUDES POLICE! A publicity photo of Johnny was plastered on the front page. The same photo was all over the cable news channels, including her own. No wonder her bosses back in Atlanta hadn't objected to her staying in Fort Worth to cover the story.

Thank heaven for small favors.

She shuddered involuntarily at the memory of the skull-faced entity that had reached out to her last night. Part of her still found it hard to believe that it was actually Johnny behind that grotesque death's-head and hellish flames, but she had learned her lesson when it came to believing in the supernatural. The Ghost Rider was real—and so was Johnny's curse.

She arrived at Johnny's loft, her thoughts troubled by the trail of bodies that seemed to follow in Ghost Rider's wake. The Biker Bar Massacre. The poisoned stationmaster. No matter what Johnny had become, she couldn't imagine that he could have anything to do with killing all those people. He hadn't injured any of those cops last night, even after they had drawn their weapons on him. Someone else had to be responsible for the murders. Maybe that "Blackheart" he had mentioned?

But who—or what—was Blackheart?

She shook her head in confusion. Black hearts and bounty hunters and burning flesh, curses and caretakers . . . she was in way over her head here. *I need more information*, she decided, thinking like a reporter. *I need to understand how all this mystical business works.*

The door to the elevator was locked, but she managed to pick the lock without too much difficulty—this was hardly the first time she had indulged in a little breaking-and-entering for the sake of a story. This time, though, the stakes were higher than ever before. Johnny's soul—and possibly their very lives—hung in the balance.

There has to be something I can do to save him!

She glanced around the roomy loft, which looked just as she remembered it. Motorcycles and motorcycle gear consumed most of the apartment, aside from a scattering of furniture and the kitchen unit on the mezzanine. A TV was playing softly in the background. The overhead lights were turned down low. Her fingers explored the wall, groping for the switch. She flicked it on and bright fluorescent light flooded the loft . . . exposing a figure right in front of her.

16

CARETAKER SAT AT HIS ROUGH-HEWN WOODEN TABLE. An old-fashioned kerosene lamp lighted the interior of the shack. Outside, night had fallen over the cemetery. Lost in thought, the old cowboy soberly contemplated the tarnished silver pocket watch in his hand. An inscription upon the watch read:

"For Bravery Beyond Duty."

The watch's hands were stuck at midnight. No ticking sounds emerged from the antique timepiece, which had stopped a long time ago. Caretaker held onto it anyway.

Just another broken-down relic, he thought. *Like me.*

A noise outside broke his trance.

Frowning, he got up and walked to the door. He unlocked the door and looked around. A worn leather duster protected him from the unexpected chill of the evening. His cowboy hat rested atop his silver hair. He scanned the grounds, but saw nothing in the dark except tombstones and fallen leaves. An eerie mist, unusual for the summer, spread over the floor of the cemetery.

He sensed hostile eyes watching him from the shadows.

"Who's there? Show yourself."

Hefting his shovel in both hands, he stepped off the porch. He peered past the wrought-iron fence surrounding the graveyard.

A sinister figure stood just outside the gate. Water dripped from the figure's sodden garments. Damp hair hung over the visitor's face. Wallow smiled evilly at Caretaker, who recognized the last of the Hidden. . . .

"This is hallowed ground," he reminded the demon. Even though he knew that Wallow could not come any nearer, Caretaker held his shovel before him like a fighting staff. He might be old, but he could still handle himself in a brawl. "Your kind's not welcome here."

The elemental kept on smiling. His gaze shifted from Caretaker to something farther inside the graveyard. Caretaker heard an amused chuckle behind him.

Blackheart.

The old-timer spun around, swinging his shovel at the Devil's son. Blackheart deftly caught hold of the weapon and swung it back at Caretaker. The blunt edge of the shovel struck Caretaker in the face, knocking him backward. The old man tripped over a headstone and landed flat on his back. His hat flew off his head. Blackheart laughed and chucked the shovel away. It clattered against the granite wall of a mausoleum.

"Did you think I was like the others?" he mocked the

fallen cowboy. "I have all my father's strengths and none of his weaknesses."

Caretaker lay helpless upon the ground, dazed by the blow, his face bruised and bleeding. He tried to get up, but just staying conscious was almost more than he could manage. Darkness encroached on his vision, yet he held it off through sheer will alone.

Blackheart knelt down beside him. "The New Hell awaits in San Venganza," he said. "I just need the contract. I know it's here. Give it to me."

Oh, I'll give it to you, all right, Caretaker thought. Mustering his strength, he rose from the ground and dusted himself off. His ancient bones creaked alarmingly, but he wasn't going down without a fight. His fist clenched and he took a swing at Blackheart's jaw. *Take this, you fancy sonofabitch!*

Blackheart caught the punch in his right palm, squeezing it until Caretaker heard the bones grinding together. Then he backhanded Caretaker with a left. The blow knocked the struggling old-timer back onto the ground. He fell across a marble headstone, his head ringing, blood flowing in his mouth.

"Give it to me!" Blackheart demanded, losing patience.

Caretaker spit blood in his eye.

A fist to his face rewarded his defiant gesture. Blackheart hammered the old man again and again, his fists raining down on Caretaker like a meteor shower. The brutal attack lacked both mercy and finesse. Blow after vicious blow slammed into the cowboy's battered face. Several yards away, Wallow cackled with glee, clearly enjoying the show.

"*Give. It. To. Me!*" Blackheart repeated, relenting for only a moment. The Devil's son had worked up a sweat, and was breathing hard. Wiping Caretaker's blood away from his face, he gazed down at his pulverized opponent. More blood dripped from his knuckles.

Caretaker's face bore witness to the savage beating. Black eyes were swollen nearly shut. His lip was split and his nose was broken. Crimson streaks infiltrated his silver mustache and beard. Purple bruises marred his leathery complexion. Loose teeth clung weakly to his bleeding gums. He looked like he had just been dragged behind a car over several miles of bumpy road.

But Caretaker's spirit was unbroken. Flinty resolve glinted in his bloodied eyes as he gazed up at the demonspawn standing over him. "You're gonna Fall," he predicted, "just like your daddy did."

Blackheart kicked him in the ribs, eliciting an agonized gasp from the old cowboy. He glanced around the cemetery before noticing the motorcycle tracks leading up though the front gate. The dirt and weeds around the tracks were charred black. He smiled, evidently pleased by his discovery.

"If you won't give it to me, I know who will."

Blaze, Caretaker thought, trying to conceal his reaction. A bad situation was getting worse by the moment. *He knows the poor kid was here.*

"The Rider," Blackheart said. He leaned over his pulped victim. "Where is he?"

"Gone," Caretaker said tersely. He'd be damned, again, if he'd help this uppity demon track down the new Rider. *I owe the kid that much at least.*

Blackheart considered the possibilities. Extracting a silk handkerchief from his pocket, he fastidiously wiped Caretaker's blood off his knuckles. His pale face lit up as he hit on the obvious answer.

"Oh . . . the girl."

Caretaker figured that had to be the "Roxanne" Johnny had mentioned before. *Dammit,* he thought in frustration. *I told him to give up all that.* The Ghost Rider must always ride alone. That's the way it was, the way it had always been. . . .

"You hurt her," he warned Blackheart, "he'll be there, like lightning before a storm."

Blackheart grinned. "I'm counting on it."

He left the old-timer sprawled in the dirt atop a forgotten grave.

A full moon threatened to expose Johnny as he rode through Fort Worth in search of Roxanne. He kept his head low, to avoid being recognized, and stuck mostly to back roads and alleys, avoiding the major thoroughfares. Chances were, the police were still looking for him, especially after that supernatural jailbreak last night. He wondered if Dolan had put two and two together yet, and figured out that Johnny Blaze and the

Ghost Rider were one and the same. He wouldn't need to be Sherlock Holmes to work that one out.

All the more reason to stay away from the police, he thought. He couldn't afford to get arrested tonight, not before he'd had a chance to warn Roxanne of the danger she was in. Once she was safe, then he could starting worrying about what was left of his "normal" life . . . if that was even an option anymore.

Roxanne's news van was parked outside the offices of her network's local affiliate. Johnny spotted her cameraman—Stuart, wasn't it?—packing some equipment into the back of the van. Motoring up to the curb, Johnny got off his bike and approached the skinny young man from behind. Intent on his work, Stuart didn't even hear Johnny coming until he turned around and suddenly found the fugitive daredevil standing right in front of him.

"Jesus!" he exclaimed.

Johnny didn't waste time with small talk. "Where's Roxanne?"

The cameraman needed a moment to catch his breath. He wiped some sweat from his forehead. "Everybody's looking for you. . . ."

Tell me something I don't know, Johnny thought impatiently. He grabbed the other man by the collar to get his attention. "Where is she?!"

"She's out looking for you!" Stuart replied.

17

A FIGURE LURCHED OUT OF THE SHADOWS.

"Aaah!" Roxanne yelped.

"Aaah!" it shouted back. A tuna fish sandwich fell out of its mouth.

Roxanne jumped and reached for the mace in her handbag. Then she got a better look at the scruffy, heavy-set dude standing before her, a box of pistons wedged under one arm and a six-pack under the other. A brown beard and Harley-Davidson T-shirt gave her little to fear as she remembered Randall Mackenzie from that afternoon at Texas Stadium. She had met the mechanic right before Johnny's big jump.

Wonder how much he knows about his employer's deal with the Devil.

"Sorry about that," she apologized.

"You and me both," Mack said.

He regarded her with confusion as she went straight for the stacks of books piled up on the floor where Grace had once been. She sifted through the esoteric volumes, scanning their spines. *De Vermis Mysteriis,*

The Montesi Codex, Cultes de Goules . . . the bizarre titles meant little to her. Where were those books Johnny had tried to hide from her before?

"Uhh . . . have you seen Johnny?" Mack asked.

She looked up from a book on spirit possession. "He's in trouble, Mack."

"No shit," he said. He dropped the pistons and six-pack onto an already cluttered counter. "The cops have been on me on me like white on rice. Did you know he got arrested?"

"Yes," she admitted. She tossed aside the ghost book and starting leafing through a modern translation of *Faust*. Maybe there was something in there she could use?

"Ever since his arrest hit the news," Mack grumbled, "our sponsors have been freaking out." He looked like he was ready to tear his hair out. Presumably he had been coping with the public relations crisis all day. "We could lose all our endorsement deals!"

Roxanne put *Faust* aside for later and picked up something on the Dead Sea Scrolls. Under the circumstances, she had trouble taking the mechanic's histrionics seriously. "Sponsors are the least of Johnny's worries."

"Easy for you to say," Mack groused, "but I've gotten pretty used to eating, lady." He cast a wistful look at his fallen sandwich, then scowled at Roxanne. "You know, all this started when you showed up. Why don't you just get the hell out of Dodge? You've done more than enough."

Roxanne tuned out the indignant mechanic. She kept searching through the stacks of occult tomes. The Dead Sea Scrolls didn't seem to contain much in the way of helpful hints for dealing with supernatural bounty hunters, so she chucked it aside and moved onto something new. A paperback biography of a supposedly famous exorcist caught her eye and she skimmed quickly through the table of contents. Maybe this Daimon Hellstrom guy knew something about beating the Devil?

Unhappy at being ignored, Mack stomped over to join her by the books. He glared at the mystical texts with open distaste. Roxanne guessed that he didn't approve of Johnny's interest in the occult. "What the hell are you looking for?"

"Answers,"she stated. Looking up at Mack, she decided to take advantage of his long acquaintance with Johnny. "Did he keep a diary, a notebook, anything like that?"

Now it was Mack's turn to ignore her. He started to storm away in a huff.

"Look, Mack," she called out to him. "We both care about him. I don't have time to explain. You're just going to have to trust me." Her moist brown eyes beseeched him. "Diary?"

Mack looked back at her, thinking it over. From her research, she knew that the stressed-out gearhead was the closest thing Johnny had to a friend these days. They had been on the road together for years, touring the country with Johnny's cycle show. She counted on that bond to overcome Mack's reservations about helping her.

He sighed and gave in. "Doesn't sound like Johnny."

That wasn't good enough, so she eyed him sternly.

"Okay, I'll go check the bedroom."

Mack left the room, leaving her alone with Johnny's spooky library. Sorting through another stack, she recognized the large leather bound volume Johnny had taken from her yesterday. *Now we're getting somewhere,* she thought. She grabbed onto the massive tome and peered at the title: *The Rise of the Midnight Son.*

She flipped it open to the page Johnny had flagged before. The chapter heading, "Blood Covenants," made her wince even before she reached the engraved illustration she had briefly glimpsed yesterday. Once again she was confronted by the disturbing image of an evil-looking young man surrounded by a cloud of fiendish spirits. The leering wraiths seemed to be flowing into the youth's body as he grinned in satanic triumph. Gothic type foretold of "The End of Days."

"Jesus . . ." she whispered.

"Not even close," a voice corrected her.

She looked up to see Mack standing a few feet away, a shocked look upon his face. A midnight blue taint seeped across his skin. Swollen blue veins and capillaries bulged upon his face, while his flesh assumed an unhealthy hypoxic tint. Even his bristling brown beard took on a bluish hue. Sulfur poisoning. She screamed as Mack decomposed right before her eyes.

His uncomprehending eyes sank into their sockets before dissolving altogether. Indigo skin contracted, stretching tight against his skull. The stench of putrefaction, mixed with the acrid odor of brimstone, issued from the gaping black cavity that was his mouth. His extra-large T-shirt fell loosely over his withered frame. A death rattle emanated from somewhere deep within his constricted throat. There was no time for any last words before his mummified remains dropped onto the floor of the loft, revealing the intruder standing directly behind him.

The pale-faced young man bore an uncanny resemblance to "the Beast" in the old woodcut, right down to the ominous black shadows under his eyes. The book slipped from Roxanne's fingers and crashed down upon the floor. She gazed in horror at Mack's murderer.

" 'Abashed the devil stood," the youth recited, "and felt how awful goodness is, and saw virtue in her shape how lovely. . . .' " Roxanne recognized the excerpt from Milton's Paradise Lost. He smiled at her, obviously approving of the sentiment. "How awful goodness is."

Roxanne backed away from the smirking killer. Suddenly, there was no longer any mystery behind who had killed the stationmaster and all those outlaw bikers. The murderer was right in front of her. Blackheart, I presume.

"You're the one who has his heart." He stepped over Mack's lifeless body, forcing Roxanne into a corner. He kicked The Rise of the Midnight Son out of his way. She stumbled clumsily over the books scattered over the floor, but managed to stay on her feet. Her back collided with an unyielding brick wall. She held up the tiny golden cross around her neck, but Blackheart kept on coming. "And now I'm going to break it."

She looked around frantically, searching in vain for some way out. *Johnny!* she thought desperately. Her frightened eyes looked to the elevator doors. *Help me, please!*

The unmistakable roar of a Harley Davidson answered her silent plea.

Johnny left Grace in the lift as he charged into the loft. "Roxanne!" he shouted frantically, terrified that he was already too late to save her. What if Blackheart had gotten to her first?

The sight of a withered blue corpse stopped him in his tracks. The shriveled face was so distorted that he almost didn't recognize it at first. Then the awful truth sunk in.

Mack?

Johnny looked away, unable to bear the sight of his best friend—hell, his only friend—lying dead upon the floor. *This is all my fault,* he realized. Mack's murder may have been the work of Blackheart, but Johnny knew that he was to blame as well. The big-hearted mechanic was only the latest victim of Johnny's dealings with the Devil. His throat tightened as he recalled all the times Mack had fretted over Johnny's safety. There was something grossly unfair about the fact that, in the end, it was Mack who had ended up dead. *This isn't how it was supposed to be. . . .*

An agonized moan, coming from a few yards away, sent a shock through his system. Johnny looked past a stand of silent motorcycles to see Roxanne lying on the floor nearby, gasping for breath. An hypoxic blue tint suffused her pain-wracked face. Indigo veins writhed beneath her skin.

"Roxanne!"

He rushed to her side and knelt down beside her. Cradling her head in his lap, he gently stroked her hair as he gazed down at her in horror. Guilt seared his soul more fiercely than even the hottest hellfire. *Please, no,* he thought desperately. *Not her, too.* "I'm so sorry. . . ."

Her parched lips moved, like she was trying to tell him something, but all that escaped her lips was a pitiful gasp. She was having trouble breathing. Thin blue streaks infiltrated the whites of her eyes. *Necroplasm.* There was no question who had done this to her . . . even as Roxanne slowly lifted her finger and pointed across the room.

"Looking for me?"

Johnny jumped to his feet just in time to see Blackheart surge from the shadows. His pale features taking on a bestial cast, the demon-spawn slammed Johnny into the wall of the loft. Brickwork cracked beneath the impact. Plaster rained down from the ceiling. A circus poster crashed loudly to the floor.

"Because here I am!" Blackheart taunted.

Anger flared inside Johnny, igniting the Rider within him. His flesh and hair spontaneously combusted. Burnt skin flaked away from his face. Red-hot flames rippled around his skull. Spikes protruded from his jacket.

"Look into my eyes!" Ghost Rider demanded, lunging at his foe. His blazing sockets looked into the demon's own black orbs. Let the Devil's heir face judgment at last!

But Blackheart merely laughed. "Your Penance Stare doesn't work on me. I have no soul to burn."

With the speed of a striking cobra, he grabbed onto Ghost Rider's fleshless neck-bone. Necroplasm flowed from his neatly manicured fingertips, contaminating Ghost Rider with its supernatural poison. The Rider's bright orange flames turned blue and noxious, as though fueled by the gas from a rotting corpse. He dropped to his knees, felled by the venomous taint. Blackheart's fist remained tightly gripped around his throat.

"I guess the Caretaker forgot to mention that, huh?" Blackheart mocked him. "Surprise." Ghost Rider convulsed beneath the demon's foul touch. His bones rattled noisily beneath his leathers. "Well, you know what they say: 'Better the devil you know—' "

Blackheart smacked Ghost Rider's bony face into the floor hard enough to crack the concrete. The concussion left the Rider's skull ringing. Hairline fractures weakened solid bone as he struggled not to lose consciousness. Blackheart's sardonic voice seemed to come from miles away.

"—than the devil you don't.' "

Blackheart crouched over the fallen bounty hunter. Ghost Rider's corrupted flames flickered and died out. Bruised flesh spread across the splintered skull as Johnny Blaze reverted to mortal form. His preternatural strength and power abandoned him.

"Listen up," Blackheart instructed. "And try to get this through that *thick skull* of yours. You don't work for my father anymore. You work for *me*." He got up and walked over to where Roxanne remained sprawled upon the floor. "Get the Contract. Bring it to me in San Venganza. And in exchange, I might spare your girl's life."

He grabbed her by the hair and roughly yanked her to her feet. Roxanne whimpered in pain, too depleted by the poison to even think about fighting back. Grinning cruelly, he stroked her check. His caress infected her flesh, causing more blue veins to spread across her face. She flinched from his touch, but he refused to let her go.

"Don't make me wait," he warned Johnny, "or I'll be forced to find ways to *amuse* myself." He licked his lips salaciously. "And I have a very twisted sense of fun."

Johnny couldn't bear to see Roxanne tortured like this, not after all the times he had hurt her before. He tried to rise to his feet, come to her rescue, but the necroplasm and the beating had taken too much out of him. Blackheart's toxin had chilled him to the marrow, leaving him cold and shaking. His head throbbed with every heartbeat. His face felt swollen. He tasted blood in his mouth. Even in the presence of so loathsome an evil, the Ghost Rider was unable to emerge from Johnny's battered form. Blackheart's leering face filled his vision until a wave of darkness washed over him, carrying away the last of his strength. The world went black and he collapsed onto the floor. . . .

"Roxanne!"

He awoke abruptly to find himself lying alone in the loft, not far from Mack's dessicated corpse. Gasping for the breath, he looked around frantically, searching in vain for the woman he loved. But there was no one there. Blackheart had gone—and he taken Roxanne with him.

How long was I out? Johnny wondered anxiously. *Minutes? Hours?*

All he knew for sure was that time was running out.

18

By the time Johnny rolled into the cemetery that night, the full moon was high in the sky. A wind whistled through the tombstones as Grace came to a stop in front of Caretaker's shack. The door was open, he noted, spilling light out onto the somber grounds of the graveyard. Marble angels stood watch amidst the decaying monuments.

He had broken every speed limit getting here, but would that do Roxanne any good, now that she had fallen into the hands of his enemies? Blackheart's threats against Roxanne echoed incessantly within Johnny's mind, along with his demand for the long-lost contract of San Venganza.

"*Get the Contract. Bring it to me in San Venganza,*" the demon had said.

"Hello?" Johnny called out. His headlight shone its high beam on the cemetery. He needed to find Caretaker—and the Contract—right away. For Roxanne's sake, not to mention the world's. "Caretaker?"

A groan answered from the shadows. Peering into

the darkness, Johnny glimpsed the old-timer limping toward him, using his shovel as a crutch. He stepped into the moonlight and Johnny saw at once that Caretaker had been badly beaten. His leathery face was covered by bruises, cuts, and abrasions. Both eyes were blackened, his lip was split open. He walked toward Johnny painfully, like every step was a battle.

"What happened?" Johnny asked.

Caretaker spit a mouthful of bloody saliva onto the ground. "Blackheart."

He's been here? The Devil's son seemed to be one step ahead of him. Caretaker's battered state made Johnny worry even more about Roxanne's safety. What if Blackheart had the same treatment in store for her?

Or worse.

"He's got her," he told Caretaker urgently. "Where is the Contract? I can't end this without it." A horrible thought occurred to him. What if Blackheart had already stolen the Contract from the cemetery while Johnny had been unconscious? If so, Blackheart would have no further reason to bargain with Johnny for Roxanne's life. He might have already disposed of her.

No! he thought. A nightmarish vision of Roxanne's lush beauty and vibrant spirit reduced to just another shriveled blue corpse flashed across his brain. Gaping black sockets swallowed up her intelligent brown eyes, along with her eternal soul. Her once-lovely face was contorted with horror.

He rushed over to Carter Slade's grave site, but was

relieved to find it undisturbed. He cast an anxious look at Caretaker. *Please tell me that Blackheart hasn't found the Contract already?*

The bloodied Caretaker shook his head. "But you say they've already got your girl?"

Johnny nodded, the thought filling him with dread. He snatched the shovel from Caretaker's hands and frantically started digging up the packed earth in front of the cursed Ranger's tombstone. Shovelfuls of dirt were heaved aside, but Johnny didn't see anything that looked like it might hold the missing Contract. "Where is it?" he begged Caretaker. "I'll dig up the whole place if I have to!"

"It's not there," the old cowboy said, sparing him the effort. He lurched forward and gently took the shovel from Johnny's hands. Hefting the tool in his calloused hands, he swung it with surprising strength. For a split second, Johnny thought Caretaker was attacking him, but then the shovel's handle collided with the trunk of the old hickory tree behind the tombstone.

The handle split open, revealing a hollow cavity inside the shovel . . . and the tip of a rolled-up parchment scroll.

The business end of the shovel dropped onto the ground. Caretaker extracted the scroll from the splintered handle. He held it up to the moonlight.

"The Contract of San Venganza," he said grimly. "Hell on earth."

Johnny could tell that Caretaker was reluctant to

hand the Contract over to him. He wondered how long the old cowboy had been guarding the scroll. "You're going to have to trust me."

"Why's that?" Caretaker asked.

"He may have my soul," Johnny insisted. "But he doesn't have my spirit."

The older man nodded. "I believe you," he said, sounding as though Johnny had finally won his trust. "Any man who has the guts to trade his soul for love has the power to change the world. You didn't do it for greed or lust. You did it for the right reason. That puts God on your side."

He handed the scroll to Johnny. "To them, that makes you dangerous, unpredictable, and that's the best thing you can be right now."

Johnny gratefully accepted the Contract. The dry brown parchment reminded him of the document he had bled onto so many years ago. He tucked the scroll beneath his jacket.

"San Venganza's five hundred miles from here," Caretaker commented. "On the other side of the Rio Grande. We better get movin'."

"We?" Johnny looked at Caretaker skeptically. The old-timer didn't look like he was in any shape to go anywhere, except maybe a hospital. And was he planning on hitching a ride on the back of the Hellcycle?

Caretaker raised his fingers to his lips and whistled.

A horse's whinny answered the whistle. The *clop-clop-clop* of hoofbeats reached Johnny's ears as, to his surprise, a sleek black horse trotted out of the mist and shadows. A well-worn leather saddle was fitted upon the stallion's back. A double-barreled shotgun was strapped to the saddle.

Johnny gazed at the magnificent animal. The Western fan in him was duly impressed. *Where'd you come from?*

Caretaker's gave the horse's muzzle an affectionate pat. "Good boy, Banshee." He climbed slowly into the saddle. His aged hands took the reins. "Figure I got one last ride in me."

With a sudden *whoosh*, Caretaker burst into flames. Leathery skin crisped away, exposing a flaming skull beneath the battered cowboy hat. Fire raced over the man's body, burning his fingers to the bones. Within seconds, an Old West version of the Ghost Rider sat astride the unfrightened black horse. Flickering orange flames licked at the cowboy's long leather duster and spurs. His bandana hung around naked vertebrae

Johnny instantly put two and two together.

"Carter Slade?"

The flaming specter nodded.

No wonder he knew so much about the Devil and his doings, Johnny realized. The ageless Ranger had been dealing with his own curse for over a century. He too had been the Devil's bounty hunter, until he'd stolen the Contract of San Venganza back in the day. *Has he been tending to this graveyard ever since?*

Johnny looked dubiously at the mortal steed. "Can you keep up?"

The other Ghost Rider cracked a fiery bullwhip in the air, and Banshee ignited as well. Flames consumed the stallion's ebony coat and mane, until only its blazing skeleton remained. The fearsome night-mount reared up on its hind legs, pawing the air with its bony hooves. Iron horseshoes glowed like branding irons.

"Try me," the Phantom Rider said.

Johnny grinned and climbed onto Grace.

"Let's ride." Johnny knocked back the kickstand with his heel and gunned his engine—simultaneously and voluntarily willing the transformation for the first time. Hellfire scoured away his flesh. Grace shapeshifted into the Hellcycle.

The two Riders raced out of the cemetery in a burst of trailing orange flames.

The desert highway was all but empty. Only snakes and coyotes witnessed the unearthly spectacle taking place beneath the lambent moon. Side-by-side, the Ghost Riders raced down the road. The skeleton horse's hooves struck sparks against the pavement, while the Hellcycle's revving engine drowned out the stallion's pounding hoofbeats. Parallel streams of fire trailed behind the spectral bounty hunters.

It was a sight to inspire legends . . . or nightmares.

As they neared the Mexican border, they veered off the main highway onto a dusty dirt road that looked like it hadn't been used since the days of Santa Ana. Cacti and mesquite sprouted in the middle of the road, forcing the Ghost Riders to weave through the high chaparral. The desert brush burst into flame as the Riders passed. Tumbleweeds, blazing like bonfires, rolled across the badlands. Jackrabbits and horned toads leapt away in fear.

A forgotten tributary of the Rio Grande soon lay before them. The Phantom Rider pulled back on his reins, bringing Banshee to a stop. Glowing red hooves pawed the ground, leaving scorch marks upon the earth. Ghost Rider hit his brakes as well. The skeletal cowboy pointed a bony finger at the river.

"My territory ends here." He turned his glowing skull towards Ghost Rider. "You got a plan?"

"Don't know if I'd call it a plan," Ghost Rider admitted. The Hellcycle idled beneath him, eager to resume the hunt. "But I've got a shot. One shot."

The Phantom Rider reached down and unhitched the shotgun from his saddle. He handed the double-barreled gun over to his modern counterpart.

"Here's two more shots," he said. "Careful. She's got a kick."

Considered me warned, Ghost Rider thought. He gratefully accepted the shotgun, which he stowed away in his saddlebag.

The flames beneath the Phantom Rider's cowboy hat cooled down, going from fiery orange to pale blue before dying out entirely. The grizzled face of Carter Slade grew back over the yellowed skull. The skeletal horse also acquired flesh and blood again. A ticking sound came from Slade's vest pocket and he extracted a shining silver pocket watch. He held the timepiece up to his ear. It seemed to be running perfectly.

Slade chuckled and replaced the watch in his pocket. He smiled at Ghost Rider, seemingly at peace. For the first time since Johnny had met him, he looked hopeful for the future, like he'd achieved some sort of redemption at last.

Ghost Rider allowed his own flames to expire. Johnny Blaze met the old-timer's eyes. "Thank you."

"No," Slade said. "Thank you."

He cracked his bullwhip and Banshee took off across the desert sands. Johnny watched as the ranger and his trusty steed galloped into the west. He remembered the inscription on Carter Slade's tombstone:

Into Paradise May Angels Lead You.

Johnny prayed that the prophecy came true at last. Carter Slade had done his duty by guarding the contract all these years—and by helping his successor come to terms with his destiny.

Now it's my turn.

19

BLACKHEART WALKED THE EMPTY STREETS OF SAN VEN-
ganza. Nighttime hid the desolate ghost town from
view. Only the ragged outlines of the old buildings
could be glimpsed. He carried Roxanne's unconscious
body in his arms. Subduing the Rider's paramour had
required just a smidgen of his power. Her bare feet dangled above the dusty street.

Wallow nervously watched the horizon. "He's coming. Can you feel it?"

"Go and slow him down," Blackheart commanded.
He, too, felt the presence of his father's bounty hunter
drawing near. "I want him here after dawn, in the light,
when he's a mere mortal."

"Slow him down?" Wallow hesitated at the
prospect of facing the entity who had already inciner-
ated his brothers. Sweat mixed with the polluted flu-
ids streaming down his face. He wrung his damp
hands together. Apparently his concern for his own
self-preservation was more compelling than any need
for revenge.

Blackheart was disappointed in the demon. "Deal with him, or deal with me!"

The elemental dissolved into a cascade of brackish water.

The moon was sinking in the sky. Johnny's wristwatch had been confiscated when the police arrested him—was that really only yesterday?—but he guessed that it had to be somewhere around five in the morning. Night would be over soon, along with his ability to change into Ghost Rider. He was running out of time.

He rode Grace though a shallow river, like a mounted cowboy fording a stream. He eyed the silty water uneasily, remembering the way Wallow had attacked him from the puddle two nights ago. His eyes probed the murky waters, looking for the elemental's fiendish features, but saw only the rushing current. Grace's wheels searched for traction on the slippery floor of the river, churning up the wet slurry. The Harley wobbled awkwardly. *Halfway across*, Johnny thought, his gloved hands gripping the shaking handlebars. He'd be glad when the bike was back on dry land again. *Almost there . . .*

A sudden spray of water struck the back of his neck as Wallow surged out of the river behind him. Clammy hands grabbed hold of Johnny's shoulders, yanking him off the chopper and under the water. Johnny didn't even have time to fill his lungs before he suddenly found himself immersed in the deepest part of the river. Air bubbled from his lips and nostrils as he fought to hold on to whatever breath he had left. He flailed wildly, trying to break free from the fallen angel's watery grip, but Wallow was in his element now, where his strength was supreme. The demon's malevolent countenance leered at him triumphantly. Long hair drifted in the current like clinging strands of seaweed. Piranha-like teeth filled Wallow's grinning mouth.

Johnny's cheeks bulged. His lungs screamed for oxygen. His vision dimmed as he felt his life ebbing away. He reached down deep inside for the strength to fight back . . . and his eyes lighted up with satanic fire.

He transformed beneath the water.

Hellfire turned the coursing river into a boiling cauldron. Wallow shrieked in agony. He jerked his hands away from Johnny, as he tried to escape with the current, but Ghost Rider grabbed onto him and would not let him go. Transparent ectoplasm blistered and burst beneath the bounty hunter's scalding touch. The last of the Hidden screamed in torment before exploding in a geyser of billowing steam. Wallow went to join his brothers in Hell.

Vengeance is mine, Ghost Rider thought. He rose from the swirling waters, the heat of his flames instantly drying his sodden leathers. Now only Blackheart awaited his judgment. *No more underlings*, he vowed. *It is time for the instigator of this blasphemous insurrection to face his doom.*

But the sun would be rising soon, taking away his power. . . .

It was almost dawn by the time Johnny Blaze rode into San Venganza. Getting off his bike, he slung the shotgun over his shoulder and walked down the dusty main street of the forgotten ghost town. Some long-ago conflagration had consumed much of the village, and time was slowly finishing what the fire had started. False fronts hid sagging roofs on the verge of collapse. Crows nested in the chinks of disintegrating brick buildings. Rusty chains were draped over the charred remains of the original hitching rails. An old dance hall leaned precariously to one side. Dried stucco had crumbled into powder, exposing the baked adobe beneath the plaster. A tottering weather vane spun atop a ramshackle structure that looked like it might have once been the town hall. Ocotillo and mesquite sprouted in the middle of the street, and through gaps in the dilapidated plank porches and sidewalks. A wagon was half-buried beneath fallen rubble. A small tumbleweed bounced against Johnny's boots. Loose boards and shutters banged in the wind. He felt like an old-time gunslinger preparing for his final showdown. The chain across his chest even jingled like spurs.

His eyes searched the gaping doors and windows of the ghost town. San Venganza appeared to be completely deserted, aside from the keening wind. The unquiet dead seemed to permeate the very air. Keeping the contract safe beneath his jacket, he recalled what Carter Slade had told him of the town's accursed history. If Mephistopheles had promised the village and its people prosperity, then that corrupting affluence was long gone. San Venganza was nothing but a memory now.

But the past wasn't what interested Johnny. All he cared about was rescuing Roxanne from the unholy creature that had taken her captive. He looked for Blackheart, ready to play out the final act of this apocalyptic drama. One way or another, the hunt for the Devil's rebellious son was coming to an end, even if it cost Johnny what was left of his soul. It was time to carry out his end of the Faustian bargain he had made so long ago.

Let's do this, he thought.

Wicked laughter greeted him, and he spotted Blackheart standing outside the old Spanish mission at the end of the street. He waited for Johnny in front of a graveyard adjacent to the church. Crude wooden crosses marked the burial sites. A rusty copper bell hung from a wooden archway in front of the cemetery. A brick wall, which once enclosed the graveyard, had crumbled to pieces in places. Buzzards perched atop shattered monuments. Dust clouds blew in the wind, obscuring the scenery. Johnny decided he'd spent too much time around cemeteries lately.

Blackheart was not alone. His slim white hand squeezed the back of Roxanne's neck. She winced in pain, but the bluish taint of the necroplasm seemed to have faded away at last. A khaki dress accentuated her figure. Her loose hair tumbled past her shoulders. Johnny saw fear in her eyes, but she seemed to be holding it together. Knowing Roxanne, she wasn't going to give her captor the satisfaction of screaming or crying. Her bottom lip trembled when she spotted Johnny. A single tear worked its way down her cheek. Was she weeping for herself—or for the man she loved?

The demon's presence roused the Rider inside Johnny. A familiar heat came over him. Perspiration beaded on his forehead, a trickle of sweat ran down his face. A burning sensation spread through his veins. Steam boiled off his scalding flesh. Hellfire sparked behind his eyes. He balled his fist as he strode toward Blackheart. A deep growl rumbled up from the depths of his soul. The change was almost upon him. . . .

"Stop!" Blackheart commanded. He smirked at Johnny, looking more amused than intimidated. His fist tightened around Roxanne's throat, eliciting a whimper of pain from his captive. "You change, she dies."

Johnny clenched his jaw, straining to holding back the transformation. His blood boiled as the Ghost Rider fought to break free from Johnny's mortal form. He glanced to the east, where the sky was already turning pink. Only a few more minutes of night remained, yet the Ghost Rider would not be denied; it took all Johnny's strength and concentration to keep the hellfire from surging through his veins. His face turned scarlet. Smoke rose from his hair and eyebrows. But he kept the Rider locked up inside him for Roxanne's sake. He reached beneath his jacket and drew out the contract.

"Let her go first!" he demanded.

Blackheart's dark eyes gleamed at the sight of the rolled-up parchment. In no mood to haggle, he casually tossed Roxanne to the side. She landed hard upon the rocky ground. Johnny wanted to run to her, to make sure she was okay, but knew that he had to deal with Blackheart first. The pale-faced youth was a cheat and a sadist, just like his old man. Holding out the scroll before him, Johnny walked toward the Devil's son, coming to a halt only a step away from the waiting demon.

Blackheart smiled wolfishly as he reached eagerly for the Contract. But as he tried to claim the document, Johnny held onto the parchment. Frowning, Blackheart tugged on the contract. The shadow of an abandoned storefront fell over the two men, prolonging the darkness just a few minutes more.

That's close enough, Johnny thought.

Momentarily shielded from the rising sun, he let the Ghost Rider free. Hellfire engulfed him, burning away his frail humanity. A skeletal fist delivered a titanic uppercut that sent Blackheart reeling. Torn from his fingers, the contract went blowing down the street. Anguished voices howled in the wind.

Furious at being caught off-guard, Blackheart came

back with an explosive punch to Ghost Rider's chin. The flaming skull snapped to one side, throwing off a spray of fiery sparks. Knocked off his feet, Ghost Rider flew backward, landing on his back halfway down the street. Blackheart turned his back on the vengeful spirit and hurried after the precious scroll.

Lying in the dust, Ghost Rider spied the glowing beads of flame scattered upon the ground around him. A bestial growl emanated from deep within him as he hastily scooped up the bright orange sparks and squeezed tightly, clenching them inside his fists until he felt the volcanic energies building beneath his bony fingers. He threw out his arms and a stream of unleashed hellfire struck Blackheart in the back.

The demon screeched as the blast hurled him away from the long-lost Contract.

Rising to his feet, Ghost Rider gathered up more flames from the smoldering earth and packed them into an incalescent fireball that he hurled at Blackheart like a Major League pitcher throwing a fast ball. The burning sphere hit the demon squarely in the face, knocking him into a pile of broken timbers. Blackheart shrieked in pain and frustration. His pallid face was scorched and blackened.

Encouraged by the demon's cries, Ghost Rider attempted to scrape up enough flaming residue for another strike. But, to his dismay, this time the fiery fragments died away in his palms. He looked up to see the hot Mexican sun rising above the rotting storefronts. Harsh white light poured down over the ghost town, dispelling the shadows that granted the Rider his power. He threw up his hands to protect his empty sockets from the blinding glare. His flaming aura began to sputter out.

"Looks like you're out of time," Blackheart gloated as he climbed back out of the rubble. Heavy wooden planks were thrown aside. His elegant black attire was singed and smoking. He wiped the soot from his face.

Ghost Rider felt his strength slipping away. The flames around his skull flickered and failed. The spikes on his leather jacket started to retract back into the garment's shoulders. A chill spread over his burning bones. Unwilling to surrender his prey, however, he drew the shotgun with one hand and uncoiled his chain with the other. The last of his hellfire coursed along the length of the chain as he snapped it like a whip at Blackheart.

Perhaps there was still time to send the Devil's son back to Hell where he belonged?

The chain lashed out like a bolt of lightning—and Blackheart snatched it out of the air with one hand. He yanked hard on the chain, jerking Ghost Rider off his feet and into the brick housing of the town well. The hero's spine cracked audibly against the crumbling masonry and the shotgun went flying from his grip. He watched helplessly as the weapon landed on the top of the slope leading up to the mission. It was only a few feet away, but it might just as well have ended up on the moon for the all the good it could do him now. As he began to transform back into Johnny Blaze, despairing hazel eyes peered from the depths of his bony eye sockets.

He had failed.

Blackheart dropped the chain onto the ground and caught up with the fallen parchment. He plucked the contract from the dirt, taking possession of it at last. The wind's ceaseless moaning took on a more urgent tone, as though a thousand restless souls were clamoring for release.

No! Ghost Rider thought. He rose unsteadily from the base of the well, his broken vertebrae clattering like castinets. The relentless sunlight extinguished his flames. Patches of skin formed atop his skull. The Rider's fearsome visage disappeared beneath Johnny's weary features. He grimaced in pain. Carter Slade's shotgun lay upon the ground a few feet away, just out of reach.

Sorry, Caretaker, he thought bitterly. *Guess I let you down.*

In the middle of the street, Blackheart got down to business. Dismissing the defeated mortal from his mind, he raised the Contract above his head. The ghastly moaning of the wind intensified, whipping up the dry white dust around his feet. His black coat flapped about him. He closed his eyes and began an eerie invocation.

"Behold the Contract of San Venganza," he proclaimed. "Come to me!"

Blackheart lowered the scroll and slowly unrolled it. Ancient parchment crackled like autumn leaves as he read aloud from the contract.

"Tobias Sanderson . . ."

A single drop of blood fell from the parchment, and was quickly swallowed up by the arid soil. Something rustled within a dried-out well, and, a heartbeat later, a frightening apparition rose from its depths. An immaterial wraith, with the face of moldering corpse, flew restlessly above the street, summoned from eternal limbo by the binding power of the stolen contract. The anguished howl of the spirit added to the inescapable moaning of the wind. Its ectoplasmic substance was a deathly shade of greenish-gray.

"Miguel Espinoza . . ."

Another drop of blood hit the dirt, and this time the spirit in question rose from the abandoned graveyard behind Blackheart. It joined the cursed soul of Tobias Sanderson in the darkening sky above San Venganza. The ghosts hovered unhappily above their summoner, wailing in despair. They wrung their boneless hands.

"Yolanda Aponte. Ezra Travis. Natalia Parker. Hernando Rodriguez. . . ."

More names followed, each accompanied by the shedding of the signer's blood, and the rise of another earthbound spirit. They swarmed in the air above Blackheart, like a noisome cloud of moral corruption. With a start, Johnny recognized the scene from that prophetic woodcut in *The Rise of the Midnight Son*. The

Beast calling the souls of the damned unto him in preparation for the final battle between Good and Evil.

The End of Days . . . Armageddon . . .

"Johnny!"

Recovered from her fall, Roxanne rushed to his side. She knelt down in the dust beside him. Johnny wished that she had escaped instead, that she had taken Grace and gotten as far away from here as possible.

"Let's go," she urged, trying to help him to his feet. "He's got what he wants."

She leaned over him, inadvertently blocking out the sun. Her shadow fell over Johnny's hand—which instantly caught on fire. A skeletal hand flexed beneath the dancing flames. Caretaker's words came back to Johnny:

Any man who has the guts to trade his soul for love has the power to change the world.

Johnny shook his head. He knew what he had to do. "You go," he told Roxanne. "I have to get him in the shadows. I've got to end this."

"Why?" she pleaded. She stared bleakly at his burning hand. "Why you?"

He prayed she would understand. "It's been me since the day I made the deal." Flesh and blood by day, a blazing specter by night. "I'm the only one who can walk in both worlds . . . because I'm Ghost Rider."

He crawled to the shotgun and grabbed it with both hands. He looked over at Blackheart, who appeared to be too engrossed in his blasphemous ritual to notice what the two mortals were up to.

"Go!" Johnny told Roxanne. Unwilling to leave him entirely, she ran to the cemetery and took shelter behind the decaying monuments. Johnny waited until she was safe, then climbed to his feet. Shotgun in hand, he took aim at Blackheart, even as the demon continued his necromantic invocations.

"Dick Ramos. Maria Cartwright. Lee Doherty. . . ."

The moaning of the wind grew louder with each doomed spirit called forth from its unhallowed grave. Growing impatient, Blackheart threw out his arms and summoned the remaining souls at once. He closed his eyes in concentration.

"COME TO ME ALL!"

Doomed spirits flocked to Blackheart from all directions, from the well, from the graveyard, from the vacant windows and doors. Over a thousand strong, the miserable wraiths filled the sky above Blackheart. For a moment, they thronged around the Devil's son. Then his eyes opened and the teeming storm of spirits began to flow into Blackheart through those very same windows to his soulless core. His body convulsed, riveted in place as though struck by mystic lightning. Fearful souls tried to avoid being sucked into his hungry eyes, but were caught in a mystic vortex beyond their feeble powers to resist. A veritable tornado of captured spirits whirled down into Blackheart, who exulted in his burgeoning power. His fist closed around the scroll, squeezing the last drops of blood from the parchment, before the Contract crumbled to dust within his grasp.

The Devil's son claimed his father's army.

His skin darkened, turning the same indigo shade as his mortal victims. But instead of poisoning him, the rush of necroplasm only made him stronger. The wailing ghosts of San Venganza disappeared entirely into his eyes as his unholy apotheosis reached its zenith. His eyes glowed with the fervor of over a thousand souls. He threw back his head, relishing his long-awaited ascendance. Ivory fangs showed with his open mouth. Talons grew at the ends of his fingers. He had never looked more diabolical.

"*Call me Legion,*" he proclaimed, and his voice now echoed with timbre of countless lost souls. "*For we are many!*"

Johnny squeezed the trigger. A blast of buckshot got the demon's attention, but that was all it did. Blackheart stalked toward Johnny with a hideous smile on his inhuman countenance.

That's it, Johnny thought. *Keep on coming.* Walking backward toward the old mission, he fired off another shot. Baiting the monster.

Blackheart scowled as the buckshot shredded his somber attire. He paused in his pursuit, as though unsure whether Johnny was worth the effort. What was one mere mortal after all, when there was an entire world to be conquered?

No way, Johnny thought. He stood at the foot of the steps leading up to the chapel. Heavy oak doors barred the entrance to deserted church. *Don't quit on me now.*

"C'mon, you son of a bitch!" he shouted.

That did the trick. Blackheart snarled and pounced at Johnny, landing right in front of the impudent mortal. With a single swipe of his arm, the demon knocked the shotgun out of Johnny's hands. Then he flung Johnny straight at the chapel doors. Johnny crashed through the wormy oak doors like a missile, knocking them off their hinges. Hitting the hard stone floor of the chapel, he skidded between rows of rotting wooden pews . . . away from the sun.

The church and mission had been neglected by the townspeople even before the village became a graveyard. The dust of generations covered the simple stone altar at the far end of the sanctuary. Faded blue frescoes depicted the Fall of the Rebel Angels, with the Archangel Michael personally casting Mephistopheles down into the Pit, where the eternal fires of Hell awaited him. Statues of the saints, now chipped and crumbling, gazed blindly from the alcoves. Cobwebs hung from the ceiling and archways. Fallen rubble littered the floor and benches. Weeds sprouted from the uneven stone floor. A toppled lectern lay upon its side. Spiders scuttled in the empty bowl of the baptismal font. Snakes slithered through the pews. No sunlight entered through the stained-glass windows, which were cracked and smeared with soot. Moth-eaten tapestries hung upon the walls. The bones of small animals were strewn about the floor. A rancid smell contaminated the musty atmosphere.

Battered and bleeding, Johnny lay on his back atop the cold stone tiles, looking like just another rotting carcass. He rolled over and started crawling toward a shadowy corner of the chapel. The murky darkness beckoned to him.

Just a few more feet . . . !

Blackheart pursued him through the sundered doors. He spared a moment to contemplate the faded portrait of his father's celebrated Fall. He growled at the time-worn fresco, which served as a reminder of what might befall him should his plans go awry.

"NOT THIS TIME," he vowed.

Looking away from the fresco, he spotted Johnny crawling across the filth-ridden floor. Eager for the kill, he closed in on Johnny. He raised his talons and gazed down at his victim with sadistic glee.

"ALL OF YOUR WORLD. ALL OF YOUR SOULS. IT BELONGS TO ME NOW!"

But before he could strike, another blast of buckshot tore through his chest. Spinning around, he stared in shock at . . .

Roxanne Simpson, holding the Phantom Rider's shotgun in the sunlit doorway. Smoke rose from the shotgun's twin barrels.

Blackheart glared balefully at the mortal woman. He stalked toward her with murder in his eyes.

BLAM! The shotgun went off again, but shotgun shells barely slowed Blackheart down. Johnny watched anxiously as the demon advanced on Roxanne. She tried to shoot again. Nothing happened—something was wrong with the weapon. Johnny knew she didn't stand a chance.

Unless . . .

A wild idea occurred to him.

"Throw me the gun!" he yelled.

Roxanne backed away from Blackheart, nervously hanging onto the shotgun. "It's jammed!"

There was no time to explain. "Throw it!"

Taking an enormous leap of faith, she tossed the weapon to Johnny, leaving herself unarmed. Blackheart's eyes tracked the shotgun as it tumbled through the stuffy air inside the chapel. A quizzical expression came over his demonic face as Johnny reached up and caught the gun. No doubt he was wondering what on Earth—or Hell—Johnny was hoping to accomplish.

Get a load of this, Johnny thought. He thrust his arm into the shadow cast by a tottering statue. A fiery skeletal hand suddenly gripped the stock of the shotgun. Johnny gritted his teeth and concentrated with all his might. Hellfire flowed down his arm into the shotgun, causing the metal barrels to twist into an unearthly new configuration. Just as Ghost Rider could transform an ordinary chopper into a truly demonic motorcycle, Johnny now converted the mundane firearm into . . . the Hellfire Shotgun.

A bony finger squeezed the trigger and a burst of eldritch fire belched from the writhing black barrels of the shotgun. The blast scorched Blackheart's shoulder, charring the azure flesh beneath his dark suit. Unlike mere buckshot, the shotgun's new ammo staggered the Devil's son. He stared in disbelief at his seared and smoking shoulder.

That's more like it, Johnny thought. Sulfurous fumes rose from the barrels of the gun.

He squeezed off another shot and tendrils of blue flame blasted through Blackheart. Noxious blue ichor splattered across the interior of the chapel as the Hell-fire *cut the demon in two.* The separate halves of the Beast flopped down into the dust. Cobalt-colored gore spilled from both ends of his truncated torso. The bones, intestines, and other entrails looked surprisingly human.

Blackheart's eyes, still demonically alive, cast a venomous look in his direction. Grunting, the demon's top half dragged itself toward the rest of him. His severed legs and hips wriggled to meet him. Viscous strands of necroplasm flowed between the bisected parts, drawing them together with frightening speed. Within seconds, the slimy blue viscera had glued Blackheart back into one piece. Confident in his newfound invincibility, he calmly faced the shotgun-toting mortal. What was one transfigured firearm compared to the power of a thousand evil souls?

Malice gleamed in his dark blue eyes. Necroplasm swirled around his fingertips. He stood poised to devour the mortal's soul.

Johnny looked up at Blackheart, unafraid. "How does it feel to have all that evil inside you?"

"All their power," Blackheart boasted.

Johnny stepped forward into the swath of shadows. Flames engulfed his face.

"*All their souls,*" Ghost Rider corrected him.

Blackheart's jaw dropped. His eyes widened in alarm. All at once, he realized that he had been set up.

"*A thousand souls. A million sins.*" As fast as a spreading brush fire, Ghost Rider sat up and grabbed onto Blackheart's lapels. He pulled the demon's distraught face closer to his blazing sockets . . . and the Penance Stare.

"*Look into my eyes!*"

The Devil's son let out an ungodly shriek as the souls within him succumbed to the Penance Stare. He tried to look away, but Ghost Rider's vengeful gaze held him fast. Murders, rapes, theft, blackmail, extortion, adultery, beatings, lies, hatred, greed, cruelty, deceit . . . the accumulated sins of San Venganza exerted an irresistible pull upon Blackheart's eyes. The brutal sights and sounds held him transfixed, as a thousand wicked lives passed before his eyes at dizzying speed.

"*You are stained by the blood of the damned. . . .*" Ghost Rider held on tightly to his prey. The towering walls of the old cathedral echoed with his wrath. Hellfire flared from the gaping black sockets. "*Now feel their pain . . . a hundred fold!*"

"Nooooo!" Blackheart screamed, unable to avert his gaze from the unending parade of horrors he saw within Ghost Rider's eyes. He found himself trapped at the center of the hellish visions, playing the role of the helpless victim over a hundred thousand times:

A barbed whip cruelly lashed his back, flaying the skin to the bone. . . .

Brutal fists knocked his teeth down his throat. . . .

A noose tightened around his neck as an angry mob called for his lynching. . . .

Poison burned its way down his throat. . . .

A branding iron seared his skin. . . .

Gunshots tore into his back. . . .

A steel-toed boot kicked him out into the streets to starve. . . .

Acid scalded his face. . . .

A Bowie knife plunged into his throat. . . .

Leering eyes ogled his degraded flesh, lustful hands abused his body. . . .

His bleeding scalp was ripped from his skull. . . .

A jealous husband blew his brains out. . . .

Callous faces ignored his pleas as he begged at a corner. . . .

Glass shattered as he was thrown through a second-story window. . . .

His best friend held his head beneath the water. . . .

Desperadoes forced him to dig his own grave. . . .

His own daughter smothered him with a pillow. . . .

A tomahawk sank into his chest. . . .

He screamed in agony as he was burnt alive. . . .

On and it went, a ceaseless pageant of crime and suffering. Ghost Rider tossed him onto the floor, where Blackheart's twitching body curled into a quivering ball of pain. The midnight blue coloring fled his skin, and his limbs atrophied, as his body spasmed with every illusory blow inflicted upon his overwhelmed psyche. His eyes stared blankly into an eternal purgatory only he could see. His contorted face was locked into a mask of perpetual horror. Blackheart had found the lost souls of San Venganza all right, and now he would forever be their victim, trapped in a prison made up of a thousand angry spirits.

Ghost Rider looked down at the pathetic creature Blackheart had become. *My mission is complete*, he thought. *Vengeance is served.*

"Johnny . . . ?"

He turned to see Roxanne standing in the doorway. He retreated into a shadowy alcove, unwilling to let her see him like this once more.

She stepped into the ruined chapel. "Look at me," she entreated.

"No," Ghost Rider answered. Demons he could deal with, but he couldn't bear to see his ghastly form reflected in her eyes. He tried to change back into Johnny Blaze, but encountered resistance, as the Devil still lurked nearby. Darkness clung to the interior of the chapel.

"Please," Roxanne urged him. She drew nearer, holding out her hands.

He turned his blazing skull away from her. "*Monster.*"

Roxanne quietly joined him in the shadows. She reached out for him.

Wait! he thought, fearful of her safety. To his surprise, however, the scorching flames *parted* before her hand. Gentle fingers touched not bone, but Johnny's own mortal flesh. She leaned toward the rippling heat haze blurring his features. He pulled back instinctively. *Don't . . .*

Her moist lips were cool against his sweltering skin. Ghost Rider hesitated, then surrendered to the kiss. His skeletal arms embraced her.

A pillar of white-hot fire engulfed them both, then quickly faded to reveal Johnny Blaze in the arms of his one true love. Suddenly, it felt as though all the years and heartache that had come between them had evaporated along with Blackheart's power. This was how it was always supposed to be.

An icy chill abruptly descended over the chapel.

A silver cane rapped softly against the floor.

Johnny turned to see Mephistopheles standing before the despoiled altar. Roxanne was surprised by the stranger's sudden arrival. Confusion showed upon her face as she trembled from the cold. He realized that she had never actually been in the presence of the Devil before.

Unlike me, he thought. He had known exactly what the unnatural cold snap signified. Johnny Blaze had felt it for the first time in a tent outside Sweetwater fifteen years ago. *I should have known he would be here to claim his son.*

"Congratulations, Johnny," the Devil said, spoiling the moment. He limped toward them, pausing briefly before Blackheart's body, which remained curled in a fetal position upon the floor. Mephistopheles knelt and gently stroked his son's unfeeling cheek, just like any other father would. The catatonic demon didn't even seem to know the old man was there. Blackheart twitched spasmodically amidst the rubble. His eyes remained fixed on his own personal hell.

Mephistopheles sighed and moved on. The unnatural chill only increased as he drew closer to the two mortals. Johnny's breath misted in front of his mouth. Goose bumps broke out over his skin. Roxanne shuddered from the cold. Letting go of Johnny, she hugged herself to stay warm.

Mephistopheles smiled lecherously at the young woman, who recoiled in fear. Perhaps she had guessed who the newcomer was? Roxanne nervously fingered the tiny golden cross around her neck. Johnny didn't blame her for being scared.

Mephistopheles turned his attention back to Johnny. "You've upheld your end of the bargain. It's time the power of the Ghost Rider returned to me." He peeled off a black calfskin glove, revealing long taloned fingers underneath. Roxanne gasped at the left hand of the Devil.

"You get your life back now. The love you've always wanted. Maybe you'll even start a family of your own." He cast a pained look at what remained of Blackheart. "Nothing more important than family."

Johnny got the distinct impression that Mephistopheles was not exactly pleased with the performance of his latest bounty hunter and was anxious to pass the job along to a more suitable candidate. Perhaps someone less concerned with sparing the innocent?

"Let someone else bear the burden of the Ghost Rider. Let someone else carry the curse. You're free now."

He reached out to touch Johnny, to reclaim the hell-born power he had instilled in the unsuspecting mortal at that distant crossroads so many long years ago.

"After all, a deal's a deal. . . ."

Anger flared within Johnny at the prospect of another poor soul being snared in Mephistopheles's web of twisted promises and lies. He grabbed the Devil's wrist before the old man could lay his inhuman hand upon him.

"No," Johnny said.

Mephistopheles was taken aback. "What?"

"The deal is off," Johnny said firmly. He shared a somber look with Roxanne. She nodded back at him, seeming to comprehend what he had to do. What he was now.

The Devil was less understanding. He stamped his cane upon the floor. A sound like a thunder crack resounded through the desecrated church. "The power of the Ghost Rider is mine!"

"Not anymore." Johnny shrugged. He wasn't letting this spiteful old man call the shots anymore. "Free will. Maybe you've heard of it?"

He gazed thoughtfully at the angelic frescoes upon the walls, commemorating the Devil's original defeat at the hands of St. Michael. The archangel's blazing sword suddenly reminded him of the hellfire at Ghost Rider's command.

"This is my second chance," he realized. "A chance to make things right. I'm going to take this curse and use it against you."

"No," Mephistopheles challenged him. "You wouldn't dare."

Johnny knew he had found his destiny at last. "Wherever a deal is made, wherever evil is hiding, wherever innocent blood is spilled, you'll find me fighting you every inch of the way."

The Devil seethed with impotent fury. Unable to contain his rage, his human mask began to split around the edges. A leathery blue hide could be glimpsed through the cracks. Gnashing fangs filled his maw. Spittle sprayed from his lips. His rising voice positively dripped with bile.

"I'll get you for this, Johnny Blaze."

Johnny grinned at the fuming fiend. "You've already got Johnny Blaze." He faced the Devil boldly. "Now deal with the *Ghost Rider*."

A look of utter hatred blew apart the last semblance of Mephistophele's human facade. Bestial and inhuman, he revealed the sheer malevolence that lurked at the heart of Evil itself. Eternal rage twisted his face into the very portrait of the Prince of Darkness.

"Don't look," Johnny said. He covered Roxanne's eyes to shield her from the horror and squeezed his own eyelids shut. A deafening howl shook the chapel.

Then silence.

After a few anxious moments, they cautiously opened their eyes and found themselves alone in the old church. Blackheart, in his vegetative state, was gone, and so was Mephistopheles.

For now.

Johnny put his arm around Roxanne. Leaving the ruins, they strode out into the brilliant sunshine of a brand new day.

The keening wind had fallen silent at last.

There wasn't a cloud in the sky.

20

J & R FOREVER.

Their initials were still carved into the bark of the old oak tree, which had only grown larger and more impressive over the last fifteen years. Johnny and Roxanne stood once more atop Crowley Hill. On the rolling prairies below them, the fragrant bluebonnets had returned with the spring. A bright blue sky, as big as Texas, stretched out above them as far as the eye could see. Golden sunlight gently warmed the happy couple.

Johnny stood behind Roxanne, his arms clasped around her waist. She rested her weight against him, just like she had on that golden afternoon so long ago. He felt a bittersweet pang inside his heart as he contemplated the promise he had once inscribed upon the oak.

"This whole nightmare started when I did something for us. So that we could be together." He sighed ruefully. "I'm so sorry, Roxanne. . . ."

And not just for themselves. He took a moment to

mourn Mack's death once more. He would always regret that Blackheart's murderous machinations had cost his best friend his life, but at least the Ghost Rider had managed to avenge Mack in the end. *And Roxanne and I are finally together. . . .*

"I know that," she said gently, smiling up at him. There was no bitterness or anger in her voice. They were past that now. All was forgiven.

He still couldn't believe how lucky he was to have her back in his life. "Do you know how much I love you?"

She turned around to face him. Her eyes glistened moistly. Her lush beauty took his breath away, just like always. "Why don't you show me?"

Gladly, Johnny thought. They kissed beneath the spreading branches of the majestic oak tree. A cool breeze wafted through endless fields of flowers. No one, not even the Devil, could spoil this moment.

Not anymore.

Hours later, back in the studio, Roxanne recorded her voice-over for a new piece on the Southwest's latest urban legend, that of a mysterious "Ghost Rider" who rode the highways by night, punishing the wicked and protecting the innocent. Officially, the authorities refused to acknowledge the Rider's existence, dismissing a certain high-speed chase as a "publicity stunt" that had gotten out of hand. A shrewd lawyer, secured with Roxanne's assistance, had managed to get all charges dropped against Johnny Blaze by pointing out that the evidence against the celebrity was purely circumstantial. Forensics tests had proven that the blackened tread marks left by the flaming Hellcycle did not match Grace's wheels, nor those of any other chopper in Johnny's possession.

No murder weapon was ever found. Experts were divided on *how* exactly Mack and the others were killed in the first place. A few blamed freak environmental conditions. Others suggested industrial pollution. Accusations of cover-ups and conspiracies abounded.

"Necroplasm" was never considered as a cause.

Tough, Roxanne thought. She remembered the frustrated look on Captain Dolan's face when Johnny walked out of the police station a free man. Too bad Johnny's big-time New York lawyer couldn't see Dolan's reaction as well; unfortunately, Matt Murdock was legally blind.

Taking a deep breath, she wondered what the suspicious cop would think of her latest story:

"It is said that the West was built on legends. And that legends are a way of understanding things greater than ourselves. Forces that shape our lives. Events that defy explanation. Individuals whose lives soar to Heaven, or fall to the earth . . ."

Several miles away, a black ribbon of open highway stretched to the horizon, holding the promise of endless possibilities. Johnny Blaze roared toward the future on his father's old chopper, carrying out his eternal mission. Forget fame and fortune, and lonely nights wasted regretting past mistakes. He had a new purpose now, a new destiny to fulfill.

Bright orange flames lit up the night. The Hellcycle throbbed beneath him. A blazing skull sought out new demons and evildoers to send screaming down to Hell. Somewhere in his unholy realm, the Devil gnashed his teeth in frustration.

The Ghost Rider opened up the throttle.

"Over time, the legends will fade.
But they will never die. . . ."

ACKNOWLEDGMENTS

When, as an avid comic book fan, I first encountered Ghost Rider back in 1972, I never anticipated that I would someday get the opportunity to chronicle his adventures myself. And just like Johnny Blaze and his stunt team, I had plenty of good people on my side. . . .

I want to thank Ed Schlesinger at Pocket Books for recruiting me for this project, and my agents, Russ Galen and Ann Behar, for making it possible. Thanks also to Marvel Comics and Columbia Pictures for supplying me with the reference materials I needed to write the novelization. I also have to thank Roy Thomas, Gary Friedrich, Mike Ploog, and all the other talented Marvel Comics writers and artists whose work on the various "Ghost Rider" comic books were a frequent source of inspiration.

In addition, I want to thank my parents, for loaning me their computer when I needed one; Rick Palinko, for letting me grill him about motorcycles (even though any errors are my own); Sumi Lee, Laura, and Katie for helping me download the movie trailer; Captain Blue Hen Comics in Newark, Delaware, and Action City Comics in Federal Way, Washington; and anyone else I may have forgotten.

Finally, as always, I relied on the support of Karen and our growing family of four-legged helpers: Alex, Churchill, Henry, Sophie, and little Lyla.

Let's ride!

ABOUT THE AUTHOR

GREG COX is the *New York Times* bestselling author of numerous books and short stories. Besides *Ghost Rider*, he has also written the official movie novelizations of *Daredevil*, *Underworld*, and *Underworld: Evolution*. In addition, he has written novels and short stories based on such popular series as *Alias*, *Batman*, *Buffy the Vampire Slayer*, *Fantastic Four*, *Farscape*, *Infinite Crisis*, *Iron Man*, *Spider-Man*, *Star Trek*, *Underworld*, *X-Men*, *Roswell*, and *Xena: Warrior Princess*.

He lives in Oxford, Pennsylvania. His official website is www.gregcox-author.com.

Not sure what to read next?

Visit Pocket Books online at
www.simonsays.com

Reading suggestions for
you and your reading group
New release news
Author appearances
Online chats with your favorite writers
Special offers
Order books online
And much, much more!

POCKET BOOKS
A Division of Simon & Schuster
A CBS COMPANY

POCKET STAR BOOKS
A Division of Simon & Schuster
A CBS COMPANY

13456

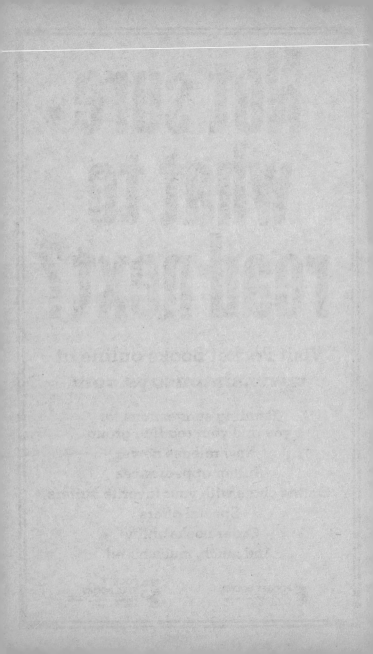